7/16

A.R. 4.8

F&P

The Babysitter Chronicles is published by
Stone Arch Books,
A Capstone Imprint
1710 Roe Crest Drive,
North Mankato, Minnesota 56003
www.mycapstone.com

Library of Congress Cataloging-in-Publication data
Deriso, Christine Hurley, 1961- author.
 Elisabeth and the unwanted advice / by C. H. Deriso.
    pages cm. — (The babysitter chronicles)
 Summary: To thirteen-year-old Elisabeth Caldwell, babysitting for a neighbor's little boys sounds like an easy way to earn some money for shopping, and her grandmother is full of sensible advice—trouble is her mind is more on a boy on the school tennis team and the difficulty she is having making a good impression on him.
 Includes bibliographical references.
 ISBN 978-1-4965-2757-8 (library binding)
 ISBN 978-1-4965-2761-5 (ebook pdf)
1. Babysitting—Juvenile fiction. 2. Money-making projects for children—Juvenile fiction. 3. Grandmothers—Juvenile fiction. 4. Dating (Social customs)—Juvenile fiction. 5. Schools—Juvenile fiction. [1. Babysitters—Fiction. 2. Moneymaking projects—Fiction. 3. Grandmothers—Fiction. 4. Dating (Social customs)—Fiction. 5. Schools—Fiction.] I. Title.
 PZ7.D4427El 2016
 813.6—dc23
 [Fic]
                                2015032134

Designer: Veronica Scott
Cover Illustration: Tuesday Mourning
Image credits: Nicole Renee Photography, 152; Shutterstock: Guz Anna, design element, Marlenes, design element, Woodhouse, design element, Vector pro, design element
Printed in Canada
102015   009223FRS16

The BABYSITTER Chronicles

Elisabeth and the Unwanted Advice

 by C. H. Deriso

STONE ARCH BOOKS
a capstone imprint

Just like when starting a thousand-piece
puzzle, a good babysitter makes
sure to be ready and organized with
all the pieces in place.

Chapter 1

"Border pieces first."

Elisabeth sighed, tossed the non-border jig-saw puzzle piece back in the box, and wrinkled her nose at her grandmother.

Her grandmother—known as Mima to thirteen-year-old Elisabeth Caldwell—laughed lightly as she continued plucking border pieces from the box and adding them to her pile on the dining room table. "It's not just me," Mima insisted. "Everybody starts jigsaw puzzles with border pieces."

"It's, like, against the law not to?" Elisabeth challenged, settling into a paisley-upholstered mahogany chair beside her grandmother.

"Yep," Mima said, nudging her glasses into place and peering intently at her pieces. "A felony, I think."

"I say let's live dangerously and start the puzzle from the middle," Elisabeth said, propping her elbows on the table and resting her chin in her hands.

"Let's not and say we did," Mima murmured, still adding border pieces to the pile. Mima adored puzzles—crosswords, jigsaws, jumbles, anything that fueled her sharp mind and busied her fidgety fingers. Puzzles, reading, piano-playing, and knitting—if you wandered into her home before bedtime, it's a good bet she'd be busy with one of these activities, even if the television was on at the same time.

Her granddaughter joined in from time to time. Mima's influence was bound to rub off, considering Elisabeth had spent weekday afternoons at her house for as long as she could remember. But she definitely preferred hitting, kicking, smashing, or throwing a ball to anything she could do inside. Funny that she and her grandma shared the same first name; just about the only thing they had in common was their bright blue eyes.

Oh, and their wicked sense of humor. They loved trying to one-up each other's remarks, at least when Mima wasn't busy plucking border pieces out of a dusty jigsaw puzzle box. But that was okay: used jigsaw puzzles sold surprisingly well at yard sales, where Mima would let Elisabeth collect half the proceeds if she helped set up. Speaking of which . . .

"Hey, Mima, are you sure it isn't time for another yard sale?" Elisabeth asked, trying to be casual.

Mima looked at her quizzically. "We just had one two months ago."

"Oh, right."

Elisabeth sighed. Money (or, rather, the money she wished she had) was a major preoccupation these days. She'd recently begged her parents for a pair of ice skates, not realizing she'd lose interest two lessons later. Now she'd decided tennis was her *true* passion, especially after eighth-grade cutie Lance asked her if she was trying out for the team. Who knew the game was so pricey, what with titanium rackets and flouncy tennis skirts and balls that had to be replaced regularly?

Being boy-crazy was *so* not like her. Elisabeth had always preferred gym shorts to dresses, cleats to heels, and the sporty smell of basketball sweat to the floral scents of her friend Brooke's favorite perfume. And she'd barely even noticed Lance, with his dark curls and dimples, until he'd asked her about joining the tennis team.

The effect was like a lightning bolt. Suddenly he wasn't just a cute guy with dimples; he was boyfriend potential! Not that she could date regulary until she was sixteen, but could he be a potential partner for next month's Spring Fling?

A guy to exchange notes with during home-room? An In-a-Relationship contender for her Facebook page?

Just a few months earlier, such thoughts would have seemed as appealing as one of Mima's jigsaw puzzles. But now . . .

Her mom kept telling her she was growing up.

Maybe it was true.

Elisabeth didn't want her parents knowing about her secret crush. They would either react with horror, insisting she was much too young to even think about boys, or with delight, giggling with her aunts and uncles about their little girl's crush. Elisabeth wasn't sure which scenario was worse, but she didn't want to find out.

All her mom and dad needed to know was that she unexpectedly wanted to play tennis. She had practiced her arguments in her head in case her parents questioned her sudden interest. Was it a crime to be interested in tennis? Wasn't it a perfectly healthy, wholesome hobby? Didn't parents *want* their kids to get fresh air and exercise?

But when she talked to them, her parents just said they weren't interested in shelling out money for a "passion" that might turn into the next two-week phase. So they'd made a deal with Elisabeth: if she practiced with her dad's old racket and made the team, they'd buy her a reasonably priced racket, one tennis outfit, and a pair of tennis shoes. Anything extra she'd have to spring for herself.

One tennis outfit? How was she supposed to impress Lance with *that*? She was joining the team to dazzle him, not convince him she was practically homeless.

But she couldn't tell her parents that, so she had to figure out some way to raise money. Monthly yard sales were apparently a no-go (even Mima didn't have *that* much junk), and aunts and uncles were growing weary of offers to wash their cars or walk their dogs.

So Elisabeth had spent the past weekend plastering fliers on telephone poles throughout her neighborhood. She didn't technically have experience, but she hung out a lot with her younger cousins. She was often at her friend's house when Brooke's mom would run an errand, leaving the girls to keep an eye on nine-year-old Kyle.

And really, how tough could babysitting be? Little kids were pretty simple, right? Read 'em a book, turn on a cartoon, whip out gummy bears... easy peazy. Elisabeth hadn't had any offers yet, but she'd already spotted a couple of flouncy tennis skirts at the department store with her name on them, so the only missing piece of the puzzle (ahem) was nailing a few babysitting jobs.

"Yoo-hoo!"

Elisabeth and Mima glanced down the hall toward the front door and saw Elisabeth's mom letting herself in.

"Hi, honey. How was work?" Mima called, still studying her border pieces, as Elisabeth's mom walked into the dining room.

"Slow day," she said, loosening the scarf around her neck. "Report cards went out Friday, and only about four-zillion parents have called to complain about their kids' Bs. So far. Oh, speaking of which . . ."

She lightly tugged Elisabeth's strawberry-blond ponytail, her eyes sparkling.

"What?" Elisabeth prodded.

"One of those moms happens to live in our neighborhood. Caroline Stewart. She saw your babysitting flier and asked if we were related. Leave it to my daughter to make me famous."

Elisabeth's eyebrows arched in anticipation of what was coming next.

"Her son's in my English class, but she's also got two little ones. Four and six, I think."

". . . And?" Elisabeth said, making a rolling motion with her hands.

Her mom hesitated for dramatic effect, then said, ". . . and she asked if you could babysit Saturday!"

Elisabeth squealed and jumped up from her seat, bouncing in her sock-clad feet.

Her mom wrapped her arms around Elisabeth and bounced with her.

"Babysitting?" Mima said, looking up from her puzzle with her eyebrows knitted together. "But Elisabeth, you don't have any experience, do you?"

"The parents will be gone for just a few hours in the afternoon, Mom," Elisabeth's mother said. "They'll be home by dark. And I'll be right down the street."

"Still . . ."

"Mima," Elisabeth said, "you taught me everything I need to know about being a spectacular babysitter."

Mima's blue eyes brightened. "That gives me an idea."

"What?" Elisabeth asked nervously.

"I could come with you and be your backup," Mima said, rising from her dining room chair. "Saturday could be your practice session."

Elisabeth's eyes searched her mother's for help. She didn't want to hurt Mima's feelings, but what kind of babysitter brings her grandmother along?!

"Mom, she'll be fine," her mother said, patting Mima's shoulder. "We'll have the fire department on standby. Better yet, I'll have them stationed in the family's driveway."

Mima dismissed her daughter with a wave of the hand and locked eyes with Elisabeth. "Why would it be such a problem for me to come with you?" she asked. "The children wouldn't even have to know I was there. I could read in the laundry room. That way, if an emergency came up . . ."

"So I'd be the babysitter with the grandma lurking in the laundry room," Elisabeth muttered to herself, making her mom and Mima giggle.

"I didn't say anything about *lurking*," Mima said.

"Mima, no offense," Elisabeth said, "but if you're hanging out in somebody's laundry room and you're not doing laundry, you're lurking."

"Mom, she'll be *fine*," Elisabeth's mother insisted. "Like Elisabeth said: She learned from the best."

"Still . . ." Mima murmured, sitting back in her chair and drumming her fingers on the table, "maybe I could jot down a few tips."

"Oh, that's a great idea, Mima," Elisabeth said quickly, deciding jotting was better than lurking.

And who knew? Maybe the tips would come in handy.

Maybe.

Sitter
Smarts

A good babysitter welcomes all
(well . . . almost all)
the advice she can get.

Chapter 2

"Huge news."

"Hit me," Elisabeth's best friend, Brooke, replied.

Elisabeth snuggled against her pillow with her phone, kicking off her sneakers and getting cozy. "I've got a babysitting job!" Elisabeth said, squealing with delight.

"This is what's huge? I've been babysitting Kyle since . . . *hmm*, wait a second, let me figure out how long . . . since forever."

"Whatever," Elisabeth said with a giggle, leaning forward on her bed to shake her hair free from a ponytail. "Babysitting your brother doesn't count. This is a *real* job."

"When?" Brooke asked.

"Saturday afternoon."

Brooke groaned. "I thought we were going to the movies Saturday!"

"Sorry," Elisabeth said. "What can I say? I'm in hot demand."

"*Why* are you choosing a babysitting job over a movie with *me*?" Brooke asked, still groaning.

"I'm a businesswoman now," Elisabeth said. "I don't have time for childish outings."

The girls giggled some more. They'd been friends since kindergarten, and there were usually tons of laughs between the two of them. A few tears too, when something earth-shattering happened, like the time Elisabeth didn't make the cut for snobby Bree Ballentine's birthday party. But mostly laughs.

"Who are you babysitting?" Brooke asked.

"The Stewarts. The oldest son is in my mom's class. I'm babysitting his two little brothers. They live just down the street."

Elisabeth heard Brooke take a bite of an

apple. "So why are you suddenly so interested in babysitting?" Brooke asked, her mouth jumbled with fruit.

"Since I suddenly need money for new tennis skirts."

Pause.

Elisabeth tightened her grip on the phone, wondering nervously what Brooke was thinking. "*What?*" she prodded.

"*Now* I get it," Brooke said.

"Get what?"

"You think I haven't noticed you flirting with Lance Thomas?"

Elisabeth squeezed her eyes shut. How in the world did she think she could hide her first crush from her best friend?

"I have *not* been flirting!" she responded, sounding way too defensive.

"Uh, news flash: I know you have absolutely no experience in this arena, but trust me, that gaggy way you act around him? It's called flirting."

Elisabeth felt her cheeks grow warm. "I don't treat him any differently than I treat anybody else," she said, trying to sound convincing.

"So why else would you suddenly be interested in tennis?"

"I'm trying out for the tennis team because I happen to enjoy exercise, and Mr. Morrison, the coach, is really nice, and you *know* how much I love sports, and . . . and . . ." Elisabeth sputtered to a halt and dropped her head in defeat. "How obvious am I?" she muttered.

"Grand Canyon obvious," Brooke answered breezily. "Earthquake obvious. Hammer-to-the-head obvious."

"Okay, okay! Geez! Why didn't you tell me I was acting like a freak?"

"It's not freakish to flirt. In fact, it's *way* overdue. It's about time you were interested in something other than ball games."

Brooke had always outshone Elisabeth in the flirting department. It didn't hurt that Brooke was totally cute, with big hazel eyes and glossy brown hair that cascaded down her back like a sheet of velvet.

Not that she was stuck-up. The farthest thing from it. And Brooke wasn't one of those annoying eighth graders who couldn't walk down a school hall without holding someone's hand. She was much more subtle than that. But she didn't mind going to school dances, asking a cute guy to share his notes during study hall, or inviting one to join her and her friends at a lunch table. Brooke was a take-charge kinda girl in general, and romance was no exception.

Elisabeth admired her but hadn't seen the need to follow her lead until Lance came into the picture.

"Teach me how to be less obvious?" Elisabeth asked, biting a nail.

Brooke considered the request, then said, "Well, you know, sometimes you kinda *want* to be obvious."

"*No.* I would die if anyone thought I was boy-crazy."

"*Hmm,*" Brooke said. "So you *do* want Lance to like you . . . you just don't want him to *know* you want him to like you . . ."

"I don't want him or anyone else to know," Elisabeth stressed, sitting up straighter on her bed. "I'd prefer *not* to look like the loser of the universe if he ends up blowing me off."

"Well, you clearly came to the right place. I *am* the master of non-obvious flirting," Brooke said, making Elisabeth laugh. "Tell ya what: I'll write you some tips."

Elisabeth grinned. "Wow, that's weird. You're the second person today who's offered to write me tips."

"And the first?"

"My grandma. She's writing me babysitting tips. I told her it was okay since her Plan A was, like, peering into the Stewarts' house with binoculars while I'm on the job."

"So everybody in your life clearly thinks you're hopeless," Brooke said dryly.

"De-hopeless me, girlfriend."

Brooke made a clicking sound with her mouth. "I'm on it."

Sitter Smarts

When a situation is unraveling
during a babysitting job, stop, take
a deep breath, and stay calm.

Chapter 3

Elisabeth raised an eyebrow as she peered closer at the sheet of paper Brooke had just handed her. "The nudge?"

Brooke nodded smartly, stacking her notebooks neatly on her desk as the girls settled into their homeroom seats.

"That's when you 'accidentally' bump into a guy you like," Brooke whispered. "When you're next to him in the lunchroom line, or at your locker, for instance. You know, like . . ." She knocked Elisabeth lightly with her elbow for a quick demonstration. ". . . oops! 'Oh, I'm so sorry!'"

Elisabeth chuckled into her hand. Leave it to Brooke to make good on her promise, producing a list of flirting tips the morning after Elisabeth had requested them. That's the kind of friend Brooke was.

"Wouldn't that just be annoying?" Elisabeth asked as her giggles subsided, cupping her hand over her mouth for as much privacy as you can get in a classroom.

Brooke rolled her eyes. "You have *so* much to learn. Keep reading."

Elisabeth turned her attention back to the list, moving her lips occasionally as she read. "The face flick?" she asked after a moment.

"You pretend he's got something on his face . . . like a crumb . . . and you lean in close to flick it off. But you've got to be really casual about it. You don't want to come off like some freaky scientist looking at something through a microscope."

"That's what you do with little kids! And collar-adjusting?" Elisabeth said, moving on to the next item on the list. "I'm supposed to adjust his collar? Why not offer to brush his teeth for him while I'm at it?"

"*Shh!*" Brooke scolded, glancing around the room to make sure they didn't have an audience.

"And you actually do these things?" Elisabeth whispered. She anxiously ran her fingers through her hair.

"Darn right I do," Brooke responded with a wink. "And it works too. Either that, or I'm irresistibly gorgeous."

"Well, since we can rule *that* out . . ." She wrinkled her nose and tossed Brooke a playful grin as the principal's announcements started blaring over the loudspeaker.

". . . and a reminder that members of the tennis team will be announced Friday," the principal said in his trademark monotone, following news about the Junior Beta Club's bake sale and the Number Nerds' tri-math-a-lon. "Coach Morrison will be on the courts at three-fifteen today, Wednesday, and Thursday for anyone who wants extra help before the team is finalized."

Elisabeth leaned sideways toward Brooke. "Can't I just dazzle Lance on the tennis courts with my athletic brilliance?" she asked.

Brooke huffed, then jabbed her finger against the list on Elisabeth's desk. "Read and learn, O Lame One," she said. "Oh, and hey . . ."

"Yeah?"

"I'm babysitting Kyle tonight while my parents go to a PTA meeting. Wanna come? Might as well get some practice before your big gig Saturday."

"*Oooooohhh*, for sure!"

The teacher shushed the girls, but Brooke pointed to the paper and mouthed her message one more time for good measure: "Read and learn."

Lance Thomas jumped backward with a yelp and smacked his cheek.

"Is it a gnat?" he frantically asked Elisabeth, who squeezed her eyes shut and frowned.

"No, no . . . I'm sorry. I just . . . you had a little smudge on your face. I was rubbing it off for you."

"A smudge?" Lance asked, prolonging Elisabeth's agony as he peered at his palm in case anything had rubbed off. "What kind of smudge?"

"It's nothing," Elisabeth said weakly, mentally cursing Brooke's list. "I guess I just saw a shadow. Your face is fine. Sorry."

She clutched her tennis racket so hard that her knuckles turned white.

"Everything okay?" Coach Morrison called to them from the next court over.

"We're good, we're good," Lance said, still rubbing his cheek.

"I'm really sorry," Elisabeth muttered again.

Stupid, stupid, stupid!

This was her grand plan to catch Lance's attention? To paw at his face like a gopher during the first water break of their tennis practice?

"No problem," Lance said, already heading back to his side of the court.

Elisabeth trudged to her side, a windstorm of embarrassment whipping through her brain. Not even the sunshine and mild spring breeze could brighten her funk.

Once they were back in position, Lance hit a ball to her, a soft, easy forehand. Elisabeth swung at it . . . and missed.

"Try it again," Lance said, sending her another.

She swung at it . . . and missed again.

"Keep your eye on the ball," Lance said, a tidbit of information Elisabeth hadn't needed since she was three. He hit a third ball to her, this one the softest yet.

Elisabeth missed it yet again.

She smacked her forehead and groaned. For crying out loud, she'd hit double digits of softballs over the fence! She'd nailed tons of three-pointers in basketball games! She'd kicked soccer balls with laser-like aim into the net! Yet she couldn't swat a fuzzy green ball to save her life? Her flirting disaster must have turned her brain to mush.

She wished the court would melt and swallow her whole.

And now, here was Lance, walking over to her side of the court, apparently to give her a crash course in hand-eye coordination. This was just too humiliating for words. Elisabeth's heart was practically pounding through her T-shirt. "Let me show you a couple of things," Lance said, propping his racket against the net, then standing behind her.

Hmm, on second thought. True, Elisabeth hadn't been this embarrassed by her athletic performance since scoring a goal for the opposing team when she was six, but it felt awfully cozy having Lance's hands on her shoulders.

"You want to step back from the ball with your right foot . . . yeah, that's right . . . hit the ball about level with your waist, and keep your wrist straight," he said, guiding her arm through the motion. "And don't forget your follow-through. Follow-through is very important." He leaned into her as he demonstrated the follow-through. Elisabeth suddenly realized that follow-through was perhaps the most awesome thing in the whole world.

"I promise, I'm usually not this hopeless," she said as they repeated the motion.

"You don't have to tell *me*," Lance said. "I saw your amazing buzzer beater in the girls' basketball game a couple of months ago."

She turned to face him. "Oh, you were there?"

He smiled, a dimple inching its way up his cheek. "Yeah. The whole school was talking about it the next day."

Elisabeth gazed into his dark eyes, her knees suddenly wobbling like jelly.

Don't blow this, Elisabeth! she told herself. *Don't blow this!*

She glanced down at Lance's shirt. *Yes!* It had a collar. Did she dare?

She gulped hard, then fingered his collar.

Darn! At least he didn't yelp this time, but he looked awfully confused. How did Brooke *do* this stuff and manage to make it look natural? And now that Elisabeth was fingering his collar, she didn't know what to do next. Keep doing it? Look at him while she did it? Explain what the heck she was doing? (Not that she had an explanation handy.) This felt as natural as sweeping him into her arms for a quick polka. And Lance was acting more nervous by the second . . . certainly not the reaction she had in mind.

Elisabeth cleared her throat, then muttered, "It was . . . crooked."

What in the world did *that* mean? Could a tennis shirt collar even *be* crooked? She bit her bottom lip and yanked her hand away.

Only when she yanked it away, her ring caught a thread from the shirt, and she yanked the thread along with it. Lance's neck came along for the ride, his head yanked toward Elisabeth's face.

Oh gosh, oh gosh, oh gosh . . .

Elisabeth yanked harder, trying to free her hand, but that just tore the thread out even faster!

"Geez," Lance said, stepping back and slapping his hand over the shirt to try to halt the damage. But his backward motion made Elisabeth pull the thread harder. The strand just kept getting longer and longer as she frantically tried to untangle it from her ring.

"Quit pulling!" Lance said.

"I'm sorry, I'm sorry!" Elisabeth sputtered, dropping her racket at her feet as she used both hands to try to free the thread from her ring.

"Just break it," Lance said. "Break the thread."

"Okay, okay . . ." She bent toward the ring to try to tear the thread with her teeth, which is when she tripped over her racket, which is when she tumbled into Lance's arms, which is when he yelped. For the second time that day.

"Holy cow!" he wailed, waving his arms like windmills to stay on his feet.

"What is going *on* here?"

Oh, great! An audience for the most embarrassing moment of Elisabeth's life. Coach Morrison had just walked up, trying to figure out how tennis practice had turned into a game of Twister.

"His shirt . . . it's stuck in my ring," Elisabeth said, willing herself not to cry.

"Cripes," the coach growled, reaching for the thread and breaking it with a quick snap of the wrist. Lance looked down at his shirt and checked out the damage: a stretched shirt pocket dangling loose from the corner where the thread was pulled.

"Sorry," Elisabeth said pitifully, biting her lower lip.

"Shake it off, shake it off," Coach Morrison said. "Lance, let me hit with Elisabeth for a while. You go on court two and practice your doubles."

Lance smoothed his now-ragged shirt and walked over to the fence to get his racket. He managed a two-finger wave to Elisabeth as he left the court, and she managed one back.

Now, if she could only manage to undo the past fifteen minutes of her life.

Sitter Smarts

Know when to be silly and when to be no-nonsense while babysitting.

Chapter 4

Thank heaven Mima was early.

Elisabeth had been hitting balls with Coach Morrison for about forty minutes (miraculously even making contact occasionally—*very* occasionally, as tied-in-knots stomachs tend to have a chilling effect on hand-eye coordination) when her grandma pulled into the parking lot.

"That's my ride," she told the coach. "Okay if I go now?"

He shrugged. "Sure. These practices are purely voluntary. See you again tomorrow? We'll only have two more days to work together before I select the team."

"Um, sure," she said, figuring she could make up an excuse between now and then. No way

37

could she ever face him—or Lance—on a tennis court again. Maybe her family would suddenly have to move to Thailand, and she wouldn't have to face them again *ever*. A girl could dream, right?

She ran over to the bench, slipped her racket in its bag, and trotted over to Mima's car, her T-shirt dotted with sweat. Lance and the others were too busy hitting balls to notice she was leaving. At least she wouldn't have to face any awkward conversations with him or any of the others.

"How did it go?" Mima asked brightly as Elisabeth tossed her bag in the backseat and fastened her seat belt.

Which is when she lost it.

Elisabeth burst into tears, dropping her face in her hands and weeping.

"What in the world?" Mima said.

Elisabeth just kept crying, hating that she was worrying her grandma but helpless to do anything about it right now.

"Honey, what is it?" Mima asked fretfully. "Do you want me to stop the car?"

Elisabeth shook her head and waved a hand to motion for Mima to keep driving. She cried for another five minutes, then finally came up for air, sniffling and rubbing the tears off her cheeks with the heels of her hands. Mima leaned over and patted her knee. Elisabeth's breath was still jagged, but she could talk now . . . and she knew she had to tell Mima *something*. But she didn't want to spill about her crush on Lance, and the gory details were almost too awful to bear, so . . .

So she managed a partial explanation.

"I was horrible at practice," she said, and oh, if Mima only knew the half of it.

"Horrible! *You?*" Mima said. "I don't believe it. You're a natural athlete! Remember when you won that basketball game right when the buzzer was sounding?"

A fresh set of tears rolled down Elisabeth's cheeks. "That almost made it worse. Everybody

39

expected me to be halfway decent. And I *should* have been! I know how to hit a ball!"

"Of course you do, honey," Mima said, still tossing occasional glances at Elisabeth out of the corner of her eye as she drove.

"But I could barely hit anything," Elisabeth said, her voice still thick from the sobs. "The coach spent almost the whole practice helping just me when he realized how terrible I was. And the longer he practiced with me, the more nervous I got. I know he was wondering what in the world I was doing there."

"Of course not!" Mima assured her. "Everyone knows what a good athlete you are. It just takes a while to get the hang of a new sport. That's what practice is for! You'll show them tomorrow!"

"I'm never going back," Elisabeth said.

"E-*lis*-abeth!" Mima scolded. "You have never, ever been a quitter!"

"Trust me, Mima, this is an excellent time to start," Elisabeth retorted.

Mima caught her eye and said, "Trust *me,* you'll feel differently in the morning. You'll wake up feeling great. You'll be excited to start a new day."

Only if she woke up the next morning to discover her family had moved to Thailand.

"Mima, you just have to accept that I'm a loser," Elisabeth said, making her grandmother laugh, which, much to her surprise, made Elisabeth herself laugh. Her grandmother's light, singsong laughter always cheered her up.

"Something tells me you'll be back on that tennis court tomorrow," Mima said.

They drove in silence for a couple of minutes, Mima tapping her steering wheel in time with a song she was humming.

"Oh, guess what?" she suddenly said. "I've got your list ready!"

Elisabeth eyed her warily. "My list?"

"Your list of babysitting tips! The one I promised you? I'll show it to you when we get home."

Elisabeth couldn't help smiling: *Woo-hoo!
Another list!* Still, she loved Mima for wanting
so badly to help her. She sat up straighter and
cracked a window to let the warm spring breeze
brush against her face. "Thanks, Mima. Hey, I'm
helping Brooke babysit her little brother tonight,
so I can try them out right away."

"Oh, good!" Mima said.

"I love lists," Elisabeth assured her, hoping
her sarcasm wasn't coming through. "Totally."

Elisabeth closed her algebra book as Mima called
her from the den.

Perfect timing. She'd just finished her homework, wrapping it up earlier than usual—her
mom's condition for letting her babysit with
Brooke that evening. Usually, she put homework
off as long as possible, but today, she was happy to
have something besides her tennis fiasco to concentrate on, even if that something was algebra.

42

Her embarrassment still stung, but talking things through with Mima lightened her mood.

Elisabeth walked into the den, plopped onto the couch next to her grandmother, and gave her a kiss on the cheek.

"Ah! I'm so glad you're feeling better," Mima said, holding a sheet of paper in her hand.

Elisabeth squeezed her grandma's forearm. "You always make me feel better."

"And you'll feel even *better* after I give you these tips," Mima said, peering through her glasses for one last inspection.

"Oh, right. The list."

"Try to contain your enthusiasm," Mima murmured, reaching for the television remote control.

Elisabeth wrinkled her nose. "Are you sure that babysitting is like it was back when you were a kid?" she asked her grandmother.

"Mmmmm," Mima said, still looking over her handiwork. "Just skip the one about using a horse and buggy for trips to the emergency room."

She turned toward Elisabeth and handed her the paper.

Elisabeth narrowed her eyes and started reading the list aloud.

"'Tip number one: Ask the parents for a cell phone number before they leave.'"

Elisabeth sneaked a sideways glance at her grandma. "I talked to Mrs. Stewart on the phone after dinner last night," she told her.

"That's the boys' mother?"

"Yes."

"And you got the number then?" Mima said.

"Mima, once somebody calls you, you've automatically got the number on your phone," Elisabeth said.

Mima looked surprised. "Is that right!?"

"Yes," Elisabeth said, trying to conceal her growing impatience as she realized how out-dated her grandma's advice would be.

"Okay, good," Mima said. "Then we've got that base covered."

"Mima," said Elisabeth, "see how the tips that applied when you were a kid don't really ap—"

"Oh, so I'm not quite as 'tech-savvy' as you," Mima said, making Elisabeth laugh with her air quotes.

"Mima, tech-savvy people don't use air quotes when they say 'tech-savvy,'" she said.

Mima waved her hand through the air, her blue eyes twinkling good-naturedly. "Just keep reading."

Elisabeth took a deep breath, then continued reading. "'Tip number two: Introduce yourself to a responsible neighbor in advance of your babysitting job, ensuring ready access to help if needed.'"

She looked at her grandmother from the corner of her eyes, trying to contain the smile that was inching its way up her face.

"What?" Mima prodded.

"'Ensure ready access.'" Elisabeth now used air quotes herself. "Mima, you're so . . . proper."

Mima tapped the paper several times with her index finger. "That's an important one," she said.

Elisabeth's smile was now fully pasted onto her face. "Mima, are you forgetting something?"

"What?"

"My mom is the neighbor. We've met."

Mima's eyebrows furrowed. "I thought you said this family lives several houses down the street."

"Mima, I could, like, hit their house with a rock from mine."

"Next door is better," she said fretfully.

"Mima! It's the neighborhood I've lived in all my life! I know my neighbors!"

"You know the neighbor *right next door*?"

"Mima, Mom will be right down the street!"

"Oh, all right. All right," Mima said with a sigh. "So you already know the neighbors. Good. We can check that one off too."

Elisabeth nodded patiently, then kept reading. "'Tip number three: In case of fire, leave immediately with the children, THEN call 9-1-1.'" *THEN* was underlined several times for good measure. "I can't even roast a few marshmallows first?"

Elisabeth quipped, giggling as Mima responded by swiping her nose with her finger.

"Moving on . . ." Elisabeth said. "'Tip number four: Find out whether the children are potty-trained.'"

"In advance," Mima stressed. "That way, I can help you practice changing diapers on a doll if needed."

"Mima," Elisabeth said, "these kids are four and six."

"Which means they might already be potty-trained," she said, "although not necessarily. But either way, that leads to tip number . . ."

"Five," Elisabeth said, returning her eyes to the paper. "'Tip number five: Even if the children are potty-trained, ask at regular intervals—approximately every forty minutes—if they need to visit Uncle John.'"

Elisabeth giggled into her fingertips. "I'm guessing they won't know who Uncle John is," she told her grandmother. "They didn't grow up in

Mima Land. And Mima, you can't possibly expect me to ask them every five minutes if they need to go to the bathroom. They're gonna think I'm some kind of highly annoying freak."

"I didn't say every *five* minutes," Mima said.

"Okay, Mima," Elisabeth said, realizing that the best way to get through this was to read the list fast, skipping the discussion. "'Tip number six: Ask the parents what the children are allowed for snacks, then make sure they eat their snacks only in the kitchen, even if it's not a house rule.'"

Okay, perhaps a bit of discussion was necessary after all. "Only the kitchen? Why?" Elisabeth said, genuinely curious.

"Two things," Mima said, clearly having thought this through. "One, if anyone chokes or has an allergic reaction, you'll be close to a phone to call 9-1-1."

"How do you know where the Stewarts' phones are?"

"Everyone has a phone in the kitchen," Mima said.

"Mima," Elisabeth said patiently, "hardly anybody even has a landline anymore. Plus, my phone will be with me the whole time. I can get to it quickly even if a kid chokes on a jelly bean in the parlor."

"They have a parlor?" Mima asked, now genuinely curious.

"It just sounds like one of those old-timey rooms you probably had when you were a kid. One of those rooms you weren't allowed to snack in."

"Well, the *second* reason to make sure they snack only in the kitchen," Mima said, "is that you want to make a good impression. And you won't make a good impression if cookie crumbs are all over the house when the parents get home."

Elisabeth shrugged. "I'll make the kids clean them up. They can clean up my crumbs too, while they're at it, and maybe even do my homework for me."

"Which leads to tip number seven," Mima said, smiling through her annoyance.

"Fine," Elisabeth said, a breezy smile still on her face. "'Tip number seven: Save your no-nonsense tone for matters of safety.' Um, Mima, what's a no-nonsense tone?"

"It's the one I'm using with you now," Mima said, faking a sharp tone and harsh expression. Elisabeth broke into laughter, and then Mima's face softened and she laughed too. "But in all seriousness, honey, it's important to remember that you're the one who will set the tone. Stay calm and steady, even if the children start melting down. For instance, if one of them throws a tantrum, think distraction." She snapped her fingers as a thought occurred to her. "Distraction like that moonbeam thing you do."

Elisabeth searched her mental data bank but came up dry. "That *what*?"

"The dance," Mima clarified. "*You* know."

Confusion clouded Elisabeth's mind for

another moment or two, then she had a lightbulb moment. "The *moonwalk*?"

"Yes, yes! That adorable dance you do."

Elisabeth opened her mouth to respond, but found herself momentarily speechless. "I'm supposed to start dancing when the boys have a meltdown?" she finally said.

"Yes," Mima said, nodding. "Anything to distract them. The more playful and silly, the better. If they start squabbling, for instance—you know, like arguing about who should get to play with a certain toy—you can hold a mock trial to determine the verdict. The Honorable Elisabeth Caldwell presiding!"

Elisabeth's jaw dropped. "I'm supposed to moonwalk and hold a trial?"

Mima squeezed Elisabeth's knee. "No law degree necessary. Just common sense. And you've got plenty of that."

"Try convincing the Stewart kids of that after they see me moonwalking in the middle of their temper tantrums! They're gonna think I'm nuts!"

"Keep reading. The next two tips are along those same lines."

Elisabeth raised a single eyebrow and kept reading: "'Tip number eight: What you do for one child, try your best to do the same thing for the other.'"

"Honey," Mima said, "you don't realize this as an only child, but to siblings, fairness is everything. A child will notice if his brother's ice cream cone is bigger than his, for instance. Trust me."

Elisabeth had to admit that Mima probably had an edge on her in this particular arena. "Didn't you have, like, eleven brothers and sisters growing up?"

Mima suppressed a smile. "I had four. But close enough."

Elisabeth shrugged agreeably. "Okay, 'Tip number nine: If the boys aren't getting along, find a way to make them work as a team.'"

"This is along the same lines as tips seven and eight," Mima said, tapping the paper. "Little children tend to be more content when they're cooperating rather than competing. If they're folding clothes, for instance, that's something they could do together, working on the same towel at the same time rather than each having their own pile."

Elisabeth smiled slyly. "I thought *you* were going to be the one doing laundry. You know . . . while you're lurking in the laundry room?"

"Very funny. The point is that cooperation can defuse many a kerfuffle."

Elisabeth giggled.

"What?" Mima asked.

"Mima, let's face it: When your tips involve 'defusing a kerfuffle,' we're clearly living in two different worlds."

"These tips are just as useful today as when I was young," Mima insisted. "Now, move on to number ten. It's perhaps the most important."

"I still can't get past the moonwalking."

"Read it aloud, please," Mima said. "I want to make sure it sinks in."

Elisabeth shot a playful glance at Mima, then read, "'Tip number ten: Keep doors locked at all times, don't open the door to anyone you don't know, and don't let any strangers know you are alone with the children.'"

"This is vital," Mima stressed. "Do you know what I do when a stranger knocks on the door when your grandfather isn't home?"

"Moonwalk?"

"I pretend he's here," Mima said. "I'll act like I'm calling to him from another room. That way, even if I open the door to a stranger—and I usually don't, unless I'm very clear what it is he's doing here—then the stranger assumes your grandfather is just a few steps away, right in another room. Same when I get a phone call from a stranger. I'll ask the caller to excuse me for a minute, then cup the phone and act like I'm calling something out to your granddad."

"Oh," Elisabeth said. "I thought that was just a mom thing."

"I *taught* your mother to do it," Mima said. "And now I'm teaching you."

Elisabeth could tell from her grandmother's no-nonsense tone that this information was too serious to tease her about. She nodded and kissed her grandma's cheek. "Thank you for doing this," she said, and she meant it. Even with a list that included moonwalking and trials, she knew Mima took this very seriously. And she took it seriously because she loved Elisabeth so much.

Would any of these tips actually get used? The odds were low . . . about as low as dancing the moonwalk on the actual moon.

Still, she loved Mima for writing them. And who knew?

Maybe it *was* time to brush up on the moonwalk.

Even older kids need close monitoring.

Chapter 5

"... and then I tripped over my tennis racket and body-slammed him."

Elisabeth, Brooke, and Kyle had polished off the grilled-cheese sandwiches Brooke's mom had made for them before leaving for the PTA meeting. Now that Kyle was watching his favorite television show, it was time for Brooke to get up to speed on how *her* tips had turned out.

"You *fell* on him?" Brooke repeated, her eyes wide as she rinsed a glass at the kitchen sink and handed it to Elisabeth.

"Well . . . more like splatted onto him," Elisabeth said as she dried the glass with a dish towel. "You know, like a gnat splats onto your face? Oh, and speaking of Lance's face, I made like a window washer on it, trying to wipe away a non-existent smudge. He almost rubbed a hole in his cheek trying to get it off. But I haven't even gotten to the best part yet: I ruined his shirt. The whole 'straighten his collar' bit? Not so golden when your ring gets stuck on it. So basically the dozen most horrible moments of my entire life all took place this afternoon. And all because of *your* list!"

Brooke erupted into a fit of giggles.

"Not funny!" Elisabeth protested, but now she was giggling too.

"Oh, Lissie, Lissie, Lissie," Brooke moaned, handing her another rinsed glass. "I thought you were ready for the advanced flirting class, but obviously I need to start you with the basics."

"Uh, you need to *stop*," Elisabeth said, drying the glass. "No more tips."

"It isn't the tips that are the problem. Girlfriend, you gotta have some *flair*," Brooke said. "Ooh, that reminds me!" She turned off the faucet, grabbed the dish towel from Elisabeth, and dried her hands. "I got the *cutest* dress for the Spring Fling!"

As she took Elisabeth's arm and started guiding her toward her bedroom, Elisabeth cast an anxious glance toward the den. "Don't we need to be watching Kyle?" she asked.

"Kyle, we'll be in my bedroom!" Brooke called in his general direction, still dragging Elisabeth along until they reached her room.

Kyle forgotten, Elisabeth plopped on the bed, snuggling one of Brooke's zillion stuffed animals against her chest while Brooke rifled through her closet.

"You've got more clothes than a department store," Elisabeth observed.

"Only a small part of what makes me so fabulous," Brooke replied, still rifling. "Ah, here it is."

She pulled out a grass-green dress with a scoop neck and ruffled skirt. "This dress with my strappy sandals? I will *own* the dance floor,"

Brooke said, holding the dress against her and twirling around.

"Oh, speaking of which: Mima gave me her list of babysitting tips today," said Elisabeth as she reached out and felt the dress's smooth fabric. "Apparently, I'm supposed to break into the moonwalk if the kids start having meltdowns."

"The *moonwalk*?"

Elisabeth nodded, her eyes twinkling in amusement.

"Why not just do a headstand?" Brooke said as she tucked a lock of chestnut hair behind her ear. "That would be less weird."

Elisabeth shrugged. "The weirder the better, according to Mima. At least if it manages to distract a screaming four-year-old. Oh, and she actually wrote down on paper that I should leave the house if it catches on fire."

"Wow," Brooke mouthed in slow motion, then added, "And I thought *my* mom was Captain Obvious."

Elisabeth smiled. "I think the take-home message," she said, "is that the fabulous people in my life give me the world's most unfabulous tips."

BOOM!

The girls' eyes widened as they heard a mini-explosion coming from the kitchen. Brooke dropped the dress at her feet and tore down the hallway, Elisabeth racing behind her.

"What in the world . . ."

Brooke stared at the microwave oven, her mouth hanging open. The door to the oven was open, and yellow goo was splattered everywhere. Kyle stood there looking sheepish.

"I was hungry," he said simply.

"Hungry?!? We just ate!"

"What did you nuke?" Elisabeth asked him, keeping her distance so she wouldn't accidentally step into any of the goo.

"I wanted some hard-boiled eggs."

"You can't put whole eggs in the microwave!" Brooke wailed.

"I just found that out," Kyle said.

"And how many did you put in there?"

"The whole carton. I was gonna surprise Mom and have some ready for her when she got home. I figured we might as well have some ready for breakfast tomorrow."

"Looks delicious," Elisabeth deadpanned.

"How did you manage to make a mess *outside* of the microwave too?" Brooke asked him.

"When they started exploding," Kyle explained, "I opened the microwave door. Then the gunk kinda flew through the kitchen."

Brooke squeezed her head in her hands. "Mop!" she gasped. "Mop!"

Kyle started trotting toward the pantry door, which is when his bare foot slid on egg yolk, sending him crashing to the floor. "*Agh!*"

Brooke rushed to his side. "Are you okay?"

"Yeah," he said, taking her hand as she helped him back up. Once Kyle was on his feet, Brooke stared at the gunk on her hand.

"Don't lick it!" Elisabeth commanded. "Salmonella!"

"You honestly thought I was going to lick it?" Brooke asked.

"Well, *he's* rubbing it in his hair," Elisabeth said, and the girls stared at Kyle as he did just that.

He dropped his egg-coated hand by his side and shrugged. "My head was itching."

"Shower!" Brooke told him, pointing toward the hall. "And don't touch anything until you get there!"

"Geez!" Kyle said. "You'd think it was a crime to try to cook a few eggs."

"Shower! And be sure to wash your hair! With shampoo!" Brooke shouted again. This time, Kyle headed for the bathroom, the back of his clothes plastered with goo.

Elisabeth couldn't help giggling as Brooke retrieved the mop from the closet. Brooke tried to scowl at her but couldn't contain the smile spreading across her face. "You still think baby-sitting is a barrel of fun?" she asked.

"Maybe we should watch him more closely next time," Elisabeth suggested.

"Talk about Captain Obvious," Brooke muttered, and the girls started giggling again.

They spent the next fifteen minutes scrubbing the floor, countertops, and any other egg-coated surfaces they spotted, with Elisabeth tossing pieces of eggshell into the garbage whenever she spotted them.

They were just finishing up as Kyle rejoined them, now wearing his pajamas with his hair damp and tousled from his shower.

"I'm still hungry," he informed them.

Brooke pointed a finger dramatically toward the den. "You will go. You will sit. You will watch TV. You will not move another muscle until Mom and Dad get home. Got it?"

"What a grouch," he replied, heading toward the den.

Elisabeth laughed some more, but she couldn't ignore the butterflies that had flooded her stomach since the eggs exploded.

Was she really ready for babysitting?

Sitter Smarts

Just as athletes need to keep their eye on the ball, babysitters need to stay focused on the job.

Chapter 6

"Did you have eggs for breakfast?"

Brooke laughed as she sat down next to Elisabeth in homeroom the next morning. "We had cereal," she replied. "It's explosion-proof."

Elisabeth squeezed her lips together. "I'm starting to freak out a little about babysitting Saturday," she admitted.

"Keep the boys away from the microwave and you'll be fine," Brooke said as her backpack flopped to the floor. "Oh, and keep them away from eggs too."

Elisabeth frowned. "There's a lot more to it than I realized. I mean, so many things can go wrong . . . you know?"

Brooke waved a hand breezily through the air. "You can freak out about babysitting later," she said. "Right now, we've got to brush up on flirting before you see Lance at tennis practice later today."

"Yeah, that's not happening."

"*What's* not happening?" Brooke asked. "The brush-up or the tennis practice?"

"Both. I mean neither. Whatever," Elisabeth said with a shake of her head.

"No way am I letting you get away with—"

"Hi, Elisabeth."

Elisabeth and Brooke glanced up from their desks to see Lance standing there.

"Lance . . . hi," Elisabeth said, hoping her cheeks weren't turning scarlet.

"I'm headed to homeroom; just wanted to say hi," he said, shifting the weight of his backpack. "See you at tennis practice?"

Elisabeth resisted the urge to let her mouth hang open. "Um . . ." she said, stalling for time as she tried to wrap her head around Lance Thomas going out of his way to say hi to her.

This was almost as crazy as when he'd suggested that she try out for the tennis team. Sure, they had a long history of chatting in the hallways, and they'd even sat next to each other in a couple of classes the year before. But that was before Elisabeth had even dared to imagine there might be romance potential. That was before her heart practically jumped out of her chest every time she caught his eye.

She still wasn't sure how Lance felt about her. As cute as he was, he could have any girl he wanted. He was just being friendly, right?

Regardless, she'd written off any chance of romance after humiliating herself on the tennis court yesterday. Yet here he was.

"Tennis practice?" Lance prodded, glancing anxiously at the clock. "After school?"

"Um . . ."

"She'll be there," Brooke said briskly.

Elisabeth shot her a panicked glance, then looked back at Lance. "I can't," she said. "I was so awful yesterday."

"Practice!" Lance said cheerfully. "That's all you need. Three-fifteen. Be there."

"But I didn't bring my racket."

"I've got a spare," he said, bouncing lightly on the balls of his sneaker-clad feet as he prepared to rush on to his class.

"She'll see you then," Brooke said, giving him a fluttery wave.

Lance winked at Elisabeth, then sprinted out the door.

Elisabeth's eyes widened as she stared at her friend. "What just happened?"

"He likes you, goofball," Brooke responded. "That's what happened."

Elisabeth shook her head. "How is that possible? I was the world's biggest dork yesterday."

"Yeah, we've definitely got some work to do before your practice."

"I can't go back to—"

"Oh, please. Wait till lunch. I'll make you awesome at lunch."

Elisabeth opened her mouth to protest, but Brooke presented a palm to silence her as the homeroom bell rang. "Trust me," Brooke intoned.

Trust her. Isn't that what got Elisabeth in trouble in the first place?

"Okay, here's the plan: Today at practice, you are gonna need a *lot* of help."

Elisabeth looked at Brooke quizzically as she took a bite of her sandwich. They usually ate lunch with a group of friends, but today, Brooke had pulled Elisabeth's arm back toward a quiet corner of the lunchroom. She didn't waste any time in serving up flirting advice, round two.

"What do you mean?"

"I mean, you're gonna be like, 'Ooh, I'm horrible at this! Can you show me one more time?'"

Elisabeth couldn't help giggling at Brooke's exaggerated pout. "I don't have to fake being awful," she said through her laughter. "I really am. That was one of my problems, as you'll recall."

"But today, you'll need a *lot* of help," Brooke repeated, drawing out every word.

"You're losing me, girlfriend."

"Look," Brooke said, leaning into the table, "we've established you're horrible at touchy-feely stuff. So today, keep your hands to yourself and let *him* come to *you*."

"You're the worst advice giver ever."

"No, you're the worst advice *doer*. That's why I'm making it easier for you today. You don't have to do anything except be hopeless. That'll make Lance have to do all the work."

"He was already helping me yesterday," Elisabeth reminded Brooke. She suddenly realized she was smiling and covered her mouth with her fingers.

"What?" Brooke asked.

Elisabeth shrugged. "It's just . . . I dunno . . . that *was* actually the nicest part of the practice— when he was helping me, I mean."

"*See*?" Brooke said.

"He was standing behind me, showing me how to do different strokes," Elisabeth said, her eyes turning dreamy. "That's when I ruined every- thing by accidentally ripping his shirt apart."

"Okay, skip that step today," Brooke said. "Just keep being really bad at tennis."

Elisabeth narrowed her eyes. "Okay, wait a second," she said, feeling clearer-headed now. "The reason he suggested that I try out in the first place is because I'm supposedly a halfway decent ath- lete. So he considered that a *good* thing, right?"

"Fine, fine, you can be a good athlete," Brooke said. "*Eventually.* But today, you're gonna need a *lot* of help from Lance. We've got to undo the damage you did yesterday. I'm in crisis mode here."

Elisabeth laughed, and Brooke laughed back. This whole flirting business was totally new ground for their friendship, but whatever was going on in their relationship, they always ended up back at silly mode. They knew each other too well to take anything—including themselves—too seriously.

"Just to make sure I have this straight: You're seriously telling me to dumb it down for a guy?" Elisabeth said. "Truly, how retro can you get?"

Just then, a guy named Craig walked past them. Brooke handed him her bottled beverage. "Hey, Craig," she said, "this bottle is *so* hard to open. Think maybe you could do it for me?"

Craig blushed, smiled, then unscrewed the top, and handed it back to her.

"Oh, thank you! I would have died of thirst if you hadn't walked by just now."

"No problem," he said. "Hey, Brooke, I've got really good notes if you want to study for our history test together in Study Hall today."

"Perfect," Brooke said, then wrinkled her nose and waved as he walked away.

Elisabeth rolled her eyes at the demonstration, but Brooke held up her hands in victory. "Judge me if you will, but everybody likes to feel useful and appreciated," she said. "Nothing retro about that. Now, go forth, O Lame One, and make Lance feel useful and appreciated."

Coach Morrison clapped his hands together as the tennis team hopefuls gathered around him, rackets in hand. "Okay, guys, I've cleared all eight courts for our practice, so find yourself a spot. If you need extra practice on your volleys, find a spot in doubles. If you want to work on your ground stroke, find someone to hit singles with. I'll go from court to court giving pointers. If you have any questions, today and tomorrow are your last chances to ask before tryouts, so take advantage of our time together. Now, let's get started."

As the others fanned out, Elisabeth hovered nervously in her spot, staring at her tennis shoes.

The knot in her stomach made her wonder if showing up for practice was the wrong decision. But Lance had met her at her locker right after school, offering up his spare racket and telling her he'd see her in five minutes on the courts. He'd smiled when he said it, making that gorgeous dimple snake its way up his face. So she'd taken a deep breath, run to the restroom, changed into her shorts, and called Mima to arrange a belated pick-up time.

And now here she was, digging the toe of her shoe into the asphalt.

"Um, we might have better luck hitting if we actually get on one of the courts," Lance said. "Singles?"

She blushed and smiled at him, using her hand as a visor against the afternoon sun. "I hate for you to be stuck with me," she said. "You'd get a better workout practicing with the others."

"Singles it is," he said, taking her free hand and leading her onto the nearest free court.

When they reached the court, Elisabeth took a deep breath and decided that since she was too nervous to trust her own instincts, she might as well give Brooke's advice a try.

"Um, Lance?"

"Yeah?"

"Before we practice hitting, can you help me with my serve?"

"Sure."

He led her behind the baseline. "You want to stand sideways," he said, demonstrating.

Elisabeth knitted her brows together, watching him. *Everybody likes to feel useful and appreciated,* she thought, replaying Brooke's words in her head. "Um, can you show me?"

Lance looked at her quizzically, the bright sun illuminating the green flecks in his eyes.

"Show you how to stand sideways?" he asked.

Elisabeth's shoulders sank. "I mean, I know what sideways means. I just meant... you know, if you could . . . I mean . . ."

Stupid, stupid, stupid! Here she was, following up yesterday's performance with *Buffoon: The Sequel.*

"Just, you know, stand like this," Lance said patiently.

Elisabeth swallowed hard and followed his lead. He glanced at her nervously.

"Okay, good," he said. "Now, you bounce the ball a couple of times." He bounced it from waist level. "Then lean into the serve, pushing into your left leg."

"Bounce?" Elisabeth repeated.

"What?" Lance asked.

"You said *bounce*? Like, bounce the ball?"

The moment hung in the air. *"Yes,"* he finally said.

Stop doing this! Elisabeth snapped at herself. *Stop acting like an idiot! This is supposed to get Lance's attention? Acting like I've just dropped down from another planet?* But she'd started it, and now here Lance was standing beside her. She couldn't just skulk to the other side of the court, could she? And *oh gosh, oh gosh, oh gosh . . .*

"You've never served before, Elisabeth?"

Elisabeth jumped, startled. She hadn't realized Coach Morrison had approached them. Oh, goody! Here was yet a second person to marvel at her charming attempts to grasp the concept of bouncing a ball.

"I just wanted to make sure my form was okay," Elisabeth said, thinking she might actually throw up at this very moment.

"Let's see you do it," Coach Morrison said.

Elisabeth felt her palms grow moist and her heartbeat quicken. This was so stupid! If Lance and Coach Morrison weren't standing there watching her, she'd just use her instincts to serve the ball. The form might not be perfect, but she had enough natural ability to do a perfectly decent job serving a ball.

But instead she froze. That's what happened. She just froze. Time seemed to freeze too, as

Lance and Coach Morrison gazed at her. Their faces wore a mixture of concern and curiosity.

She squeezed her toes into the soles of her shoes, bit her lip to steady her quavering chin, then said in barely a whisper, "I'm sorry. I'm just . . . Is it okay if I take a quick break?"

Before Coach Morrison could even answer, Elisabeth started trotting toward the bench, her heart galloping against her T-shirt like a runaway horse. Once she reached the bench, she flopped down on it and pitched forward, her forearms braced against her knees.

"You okay?" Coach Morrison called over.

Elisabeth managed to nod. "I'm okay," she finally called back. "I guess the heat got to me."

Yeah, it must have been all of 72 degrees outside. Whew! Maybe the coach should have poured ice water over her head to avoid heatstroke.

Well, just in case the coach had any doubt from the day earlier, Elisabeth was pretty sure he was now clear about what kind of addition she'd make to the tennis team.

Funny . . . this moment was the first she was even considering the reason she was here: to try out for the tennis team. Something she might really love. Something she could be good at. If she hadn't been so busy flirting with Lance, she might have spent a moment or two concentrating on her actual goal.

Keep your eye on the ball, Lance had told her just the day before. It was obvious advice she'd first heard years ago. But Elisabeth realized that returning to the basics was the most important thing she could do right now. She'd taken her eye off the ball when she forgot why she was on the tennis court in the first place.

And it would probably cost her a spot on the tennis team.

Sitter Smarts

Experience counts! Turn to others for babysitting help when needed.

Chapter 7

At least she was more subtle this time.

Instead of bursting into tears the moment she got into Mima's car like she'd done the day before, Elisabeth simply gulped down the knot in her throat and dabbed her moist eyes.

At least she *thought* she was being subtle.

"What's wrong?" Mima asked as she drove out of the parking lot.

Darn!

Elisabeth shook her head briskly, both to signal to Mima that she was okay and to jostle loose the ridiculousness that was clogging up her brain. Crying on the way home for the second day in a row—and over a boy, of all things—was *so* not her style. It was all Elisabeth could do to sit patiently in the lunchroom when her friends were whining over their crushes. *Get over it,* she felt like telling them, amazed that otherwise smart and normal girls could get caught up in the drama. Now, she was telling it to herself: *Get over it, Elisabeth. Quit being a drama queen. Quit freaking out your grandma. Quit being boy-crazy. Quit listening to Brooke's advice.*

"You're not okay," Mima insisted as she drove. "You're in tears for the second day in a row. What in the world is going on at those tennis practices?"

Very little tennis, actually, Elisabeth thought. *I'm too busy making a fool out of myself to manage to even hit the ball.*

The irony was overwelming. It was sports that had made Lance notice her. She was good at them, and he thought that was cool. Now, in the space of only two days, she's managed to undo eight years' worth of trophies and pennants, convincing Lance (and everyone else on the tennis courts, including Coach Morrison) that a monkey could handle a racket better than she could. No . . . that was an insult to monkeys. An *elephant* could handle a racket better than she could.

Elisabeth peered into the glare of the sun through tear-stained eyes and noticed Mima wasn't driving the usual route.

"Where are we going?" she asked.

Mima smiled. "I'm in the mood for a treat."

"A treat?"

Mima took a right at the stop sign. A couple of blocks down the street was a giant ice cream scoop looming over a shop painted in sherbet-colored stripes. All through elementary school, Mima and Elisabeth had made at least weekly visits to Pop's Ice Cream Shoppe, listening to the bell on the door clang as they walked into the hyper-chilled air. They would sit on swirly vinyl stools to place their orders, then carry their cones to one of the little pastel-colored tables with heart-shaped chairs, licking their ice cream as blenders whirred in the background. Little kids with chocolate-smudged faces gathered at a claw machine full of small stuffed animals. No one ever seemed to snag a toy, but that never stopped anyone, including Elisabeth, from trying.

Mima usually limited Elisabeth to a single quarter, a single try, but occasionally that second gleaming quarter would appear from her purse, making Elisabeth feel like the richest person on earth. Two tries for a teeny stuffed kitten in a single afternoon? Life got no better than that, no matter how many times she left empty-handed.

But as much as Elisabeth loved the memories, all she wanted to do right now was sulk in silence. "Ice cream, Mima?" Elisabeth asked as her grandmother parked the car.

"It's gotten so hot outside," Mima said, fanning herself for extra effect after pulling the key out of the ignition. "This spring weather has snuck up on me. You don't mind a quick stop, do you?"

Mima was already getting out of the car. Elisabeth sighed and followed her.

"Hmm," Mima said as she sat on a stool, peering down at the oversized tubs of ice cream in the freezer below them.

"Mima, you always order the same thing," Elisabeth said quietly, anxious not to draw attention to herself and her tear-stained eyes.

"You know what? I'm in an adventurous mood. I think I'll go for a scoop of Rocky Road today."

"Cup or cone?" the teenager asked.

"Cone," Mima said.

The teenager's gaze moved to Elisabeth. "The same," Elisabeth said staring at the floor, eager to move things along.

"Rocky Road?" Mima asked. "I thought you hated nuts."

"They're fine," she said under her breath.

"And marshmallows!" Mima persisted. "You hate nuts and marshmallows! What are you thinking, silly?"

That I really just want to crawl into a corner and be alone, Elisabeth thought miserably. Why, oh why, had she had to get all weepy in the car? If she had kept it together, she'd be home by now.

The teenager hovered uncertainly over the vat of Rocky Road. "It's fine," Elisabeth told her. Mima looked unconvinced, but thankfully, the teenager continued with the order, handing each of them a Rocky Road ice cream cone.

"*Mmm,*" Mima said, taking a lick before handing the cone to Elisabeth so she could fumble with change to pay for the ice cream. *Why did she have to use change?* Elisabeth whined to herself.

"Let's see . . . just one more dime . . ." Mima said, digging into the bottom of her purse.

"We've got a change jar for people who are a little short," the teenager said, gesturing toward a polka-dot-painted plastic container.

"No, no, it's in here somewhere," Mima said, digging deeper into her purse as Elisabeth dug her nails deeper into her palms.

Finally, a dusty dime emerged from the bottom of her purse. "Here we go!" Mima said, handing it to the teenager. "It was about time I got rid of some change."

Mima, please, Elisabeth moaned to herself.

Mima got off her stool and started walking toward a table.

"You don't want to just take them to go?" Elisabeth asked, but her grandmother was already settling into a seat and waving away the question. Elisabeth followed her reluctantly.

"So," Mima said as they pushed their chairs into the table. "Want to tell me what's been going on the last couple of days?"

Elisabeth studied her grandmother's crinkly eyes for a moment, then felt a wave of shame wash over her. Mima was truly worried about her. She was desperate to ease her granddaughter's pain, to help solve a problem, to bring a smile to her face with an ice cream run. She would do anything for Elisabeth, and all Elisabeth could offer in return was a jumbo scoop of embarrassment at being treated like a little kid. Elisabeth wasn't just a horrible flirter and tennis player; she was a horrible granddaughter—and to the world's sweetest grandmother.

True, Elisabeth was tied up in knots from taking Brooke's advice, and true, Kyle's egg fiasco had made her wonder whether she was really ready for her first solo babysitting job. But no matter how nervous she was, no matter how huge her problems seemed, she decided then and there that she would never, ever take her stress out on Mima. She pinched her lips together and resolved to shape up. If Mima wanted to know what was wrong, she would tell her, even if it was embarrassing.

Elisabeth collected her thoughts for a moment, then leaned into the table. "Mima," she said in a lowered voice, "how did you and Grandpa get together?"

Mima's brows knitted together. "You mean, how did we meet?"

"No, I know you met in high school," Elisabeth

said. "I mean . . . I mean, how did you know he liked you? Or how did you know you liked him? How did you get to be . . ."

"An item?" Mima ventured.

Elisabeth laughed at her retro-speak. "Okay," she said. "How did you get to be an item?"

Mima's free hand waved breezily through the air. "Oh, girls can tell when a fellow is interested," she said.

"Can they?" Elisabeth asked.

Mima's eyes searched Elisabeth's. "So . . ." she said slowly, "there's a boy you like at these tennis practices?"

Elisabeth felt her face flush. "It's nothing," she murmured, staring at her lap.

"What's his name?" Mima prodded, and Elisabeth couldn't help smiling.

"His name is Cute Guy Who Will Never Like Me Because I've Convinced Him I'm the Biggest Dweeb on the Face of the Earth."

"Let's call him Cute for short," Mima said,

warming to the subject. "He's the reason you're trying out for the tennis team?"

Elisabeth nibbled a nail. "I mean, not the *only* reason . . ."

Mima nodded, processing the information.

"But it doesn't matter," Elisabeth added, "because I'm awful at tennis, and I'm awful at flirting, so it's totally a mute point."

Mima tried unsuccessfully to conceal a smile. "'Moot,'" she corrected her granddaughter. "A moot point."

"See? I'm even a disaster at vocabulary."

Her grandma reached over and squeezed her hand. "You're not a disaster at anything. So, how long have you had a crush on this boy?"

Panic flooded Elisabeth's eyes. "Mima, you can't breathe a word of this to Mom."

"Scout's honor," she said, holding up her palm.

"Well," Elisabeth said, "the funny thing is I didn't even know I *did* have a crush on him. He's just a friend, you know? I mean, a really cute, really funny, really sweet friend. But a friend. Then, a couple of weeks ago, he started kinda hinting that it would be cool if I tried out for the tennis team. He acted like he really wanted me to. Then I thought, like, *Omigosh, maybe he likes me!* I mean, more than just as a friend. I know I'm not old enough to date or anything, but . . ."

"Honey, it's okay to like a boy," Mima said gently. "But where's my strong, confident girl? Why are you acting like you should throw him a parade because he noticed you? Of *course* he noticed you. You are fabulous. He should feel lucky that *you* noticed *him* . . . and he probably does."

Elisabeth shook her head. Such a grandma-like thing to say. "You don't get it, Mima. I'm not the kind of girl who guys notice."

"Well, *he* noticed you."

"True. So I didn't want to blow it. That's why Brooke was helping me. She knows about this kind of stuff. She gave me some tips on how to act around him—stuff like wiping imaginary smudges off his face, or straightening his collar when it didn't need straightening, or playing dumb on the tennis court, which, trust me, required no effort on my part whatsoever, or—"

"Elisabeth!" Mima said, her bright blue eyes widening. "I love Brooke, but I don't know what she was thinking. You followed that awful advice? This isn't like you at all!"

Elisabeth nodded sadly. "That was kinda the point, Mima. I was awful at it."

"You were awful at trying to be someone you *aren't*," Mima said. "You're just fine at being your-self. And that's who this boy noticed."

"I know, Mima, but . . ."

"Tell me everything."

Elisabeth and her grandma glanced up to see Brooke standing over their shoulders, breathless from rushing over.

"Brooke!" Elisabeth said. "What are you doing here?"

"Saw your Mima's car in the parking lot. Hi, Mima. I talked my mom into stopping. She's ordering ice cream." Brooke nodded in her mom's direction. Elisabeth caught her eye and smiled. They shared a little wave.

Elisabeth was about to offer Brooke a seat, but she was already pulling up a chair and settling in.

"Did you tell your grandma about Lance?" Brooke said, pushing a lock of brown hair behind her ear as she shifted in her seat to face Mima. "See, there's this guy at school who's really cute, and a couple of weeks ago—"

"I think I'm up to speed," Mima said.

"And if she *hadn't* been?" Elisabeth said to Brooke. "What a big mouth! And we are *so* not talking about this when your mom comes over!"

"Then hurry up and tell me now," Brooke said. "How did it go?"

Elisabeth squeezed her eyes shut in exasperation, then popped them back open. "It went horribly! It was a disaster! You give the worst tips ever!"

Brooke leaned closer to Mima and murmured mock-confidentially, "It's all in the execution."

Mima and Elisabeth couldn't help but laugh.

"You told her to wipe imaginary smudges off his face?" Mima said. "You told her to play dumb on the tennis court? Brooke, sweetheart, what kind of advice is that?"

Brooke shrugged. "Desperate times call for desperate measures."

"I wasn't desperate!" Elisabeth said, laughing through her words. "I was just fine before you started twisting me in knots."

"So did you ruin any of his clothes today?" Brooke asked with a giggle. Elisabeth joined in with her friend's laughter and pretended to swat her.

"I ruined any chance of making the tennis team," she answered, still smiling. "And I'm pretty sure that I convinced Lance he'd have more fun hanging around his orthodontist than me. So thanks for that."

"Okay, here's what we'll do tomorrow," Brooke said.

Elisabeth's index finger shot to her mouth. Brooke's mom was walking to the table, two ice cream cones in hand.

"Elisabeth, hi, honey!" her mom said brightly. "And hello, Mrs. Thompson! So nice to see you! So: What were you girls talking about?"

"Babysitting," Elisabeth blurted, giving Brooke a look as Brooke's mom pulled up a chair.

"Right," Brooke said, taking one of the cones from her mom. "Elisabeth is excited about her first real babysitting job after spending last night mopping egg yolk off the floor at our house. Hopefully her job will be as successful as that!"

"Egg yolk?" Mima asked.

"Long story," Elisabeth told her.

"Oh, she'll do just fine," Brooke's mom said.

"I've been giving her some tips," Mima said.

"Sure hope they aren't the worst tips ever," Brooke murmured under her breath in a sing-song voice. Elisabeth rolled her eyes.

"Oh, don't worry. You'll be a natural," Brooke's mother assured her. "Hopefully not *all* kids are as rambunctious as Kyle. Just keep them away from the eggs."

"What about eggs?" Mima asked again.

"It's nothing," Elisabeth assured her. "Let's just say I got a crash course in boys last night at Brooke's house."

"Yep, she's learning plenty about boys—learning from the best," Brooke said, still using her singsong voice. This time Elisabeth shot her an urgent cut-it-out glare.

"She'll do just fine if she follows the tips," Mima said, tousling a lock of Brooke's hair playfully. "*My* tips."

Brooke's mom scanned their faces one by one. "Why do I get the feeling there's more to this conversation than you're letting on?"

Brooke and Elisabeth started giggling, then Mima joined in.

"*What?*" Brooke's mother demanded, now laughing herself.

"Nothing, nothing," Elisabeth insisted, her cheeks rosy. "Just do me a favor: Don't give me any tips."

Sitter Smarts

Be yourself. It's exhausting to try to be something you aren't, and kids can tell if you're not being your true self.

Chapter 8

". . . but if she didn't let me give her the tips, she was threatening to hover in the laundry room while I babysat."

Lance laughed lightly, the green flecks in his eyes sparkling as a breeze nudged a dark lock from his forehead.

Elisabeth took a deep breath of the jasmine-scented spring air and crossed her legs at the ankles. She couldn't believe it: As she told Lance about her upcoming babysitting job, Elisabeth was actually having a normal conversation with him, just like she used to! It felt so good. Maybe she'd ruined any chance for romance . . . but she had her friend back!

And it was the friendship, she knew now, that she cared about. It was part of her motivation for gathering every ounce of courage to get back on the tennis court. She'd decided at the ice cream parlor the day before that if she didn't make the tennis team, so be it. But she wouldn't *slink* away. She wouldn't *run* away. That was *so* not her style.

She'd show up for practice, and she'd give it all she had. What's more, she'd actually concentrate on the sport this time. No more silly games. No more pretending to be somebody she wasn't. No more ridiculous distractions.

As they sat on the bench waiting for practice to start, Elisabeth knew for sure she'd made the right decision. She hadn't felt this lighthearted in days.

"Hovering in the laundry room," Lance repeated to himself, seeming to enjoy the mental picture he was forming. "Kinda like Cyrano de Bergerac."

Elisabeth nodded cheerfully, recalling the classic play they'd read the year before in language arts class about a man who pulls the strings for his friend, feeding him lines and otherwise working behind the scenes to help the friend win over his true love. "There have been a *lot* of Cyrano de Bergeracs in my life lately," Elisabeth said. If Lance only knew.

A warm breeze brushed against their faces as other tennis team hopefuls began to gather, talking casually among themselves as their rackets dangled by their sides. Elisabeth glanced at Lance, did a double-take, then smiled as she realized that the breeze had actually blown a sliver of a leaf onto his cheek.

She leaned forward, wrinkled her nose, and casually flecked it off.

"You had something on your face," she said, holding Lance's gaze.

"Thanks," he said, that crazy-cute dimple settling into his cheek.

That was it. A simple, relaxed moment. Just like her swings and her serves would be authentic and relaxed when tennis practice began in a few minutes. No Cyrano de Bergerac pulling her strings.

Mima's words echoed in her mind: *You're just fine at being yourself.*

It had sounded like grandma-speak when she'd heard it the day before. But now she was starting to believe it.

"Much better!"

Elisabeth tossed a smile over her shoulder to Coach Morrison as he gave her a thumbs-up from the side of the court. She was hitting with a different group—she figured Lance could use a real practice for a change—and she was working hard on the follow-through of her ground strokes.

"Not bad!" her doubles partner, Hayden, told her as she got into position to return a serve.

"Thanks."

Elisabeth didn't even mind that he sounded pleasantly surprised. The rest of the tennis team hopefuls had no doubt gotten the memo that she'd been a spectacular flop for the first two practices. "That's okay," she told herself quietly as she bounced lightly on her sneakers awaiting the serve. "Nothing better than low expectations."

The serve sailed into the far-right corner of the service box. Mentally noting Coach Morrison's instructions, she stepped back with her right foot, leaned into the ball with a firm wrist, hit it in the center of the racket, and completed the half-circle motion with her arm.

"Now that's follow-through!" the coach yelled.

Elisabeth was smiling so broadly that she scrambled momentarily as the ball soared back at her.

"Split step!" the coach barked. "Split step!"

She couldn't recover in time, and Hayden ended up running behind her to return the ball.

She ducked down as the green ball whizzed over her head.

"You've got to stay focused," Hayden told her, and Elisabeth nodded smartly, remembering her split step this time as she stared at the ball that was about to come sailing back at them.

She'd be ready this time.

She wasn't perfect—far from it—but for the next fifty minutes, she would be focused. She would give it her all.

And tomorrow, when Coach Morrison announced the names of the tennis team, she'd hold her head high, whatever the outcome.

"How'd it go?"

Elisabeth slipped her racket into the bag and zipped it shut. "Better," she told Lance. "I actually started kinda getting the hang of it today."

He took a swig from a water bottle. "I knew you would," he said.

Elisabeth surveyed the other players as they milled about, packing up their gear. "I don't know," she said. "A lot of these guys have way more experience than I do."

Coach Morrison offered a high five as he walked past her. "Big improvement today, Caldwell," he told her. "Solid effort."

Lance smiled as the coach passed them. "It took guts to get back out here today," he told Elisabeth.

She cringed. "I was that awful?"

He shook his head unconvincingly. "*Nah.* I mean, not totally. I mean . . . uh . . . okay, yeah, you were pretty awful."

They laughed together.

"Well," she said, "nothing to do now but wait to see if I was un-awful enough today to make the team. Then, on to my next challenge. I plan to be the Venus Williams of the babysitting circuit, you know."

"I think you can totally nail that."

"Or at least make a solid effort," Elisabeth said, imitating Coach Morrison's deep voice and making them laugh again.

"How old are these kids you're babysitting?" Lance asked.

"Six and four."

"Jenga." Lance pointed at her for emphasis. "Bring Jenga. I loved that game when I was little. Coulda played it for days if my mom had let me."

Elisabeth considered the advice, then nodded gamely. "Beats doing the moonwalk. That was another of my grandma's tips: I'm apparently supposed to break out in a moonwalk to distract the kids if things get rowdy."

Lance sputtered with laughter. "You're not serious."

"Oh, I'm serious," Elisabeth said, then dropped her tennis bag onto the bench and showed him a couple of her moves on the spot.

Lance's eyes twinkled as he nodded appreciatively. "That would totally distract me. Of course,

Jenga's another option if you want to avoid making them think you're off-the-charts cray-cray."

"I can pull off cray-cray," Elisabeth assured him. "But I'll bring Jenga too, just as a backup."

"Then you're set," Lance said.

Right.

She was set.

Come to babysitting jobs prepared.

Chapter 9

"... oh, and Jenga. He told me to bring Jenga to the Stewarts' house tomorrow."

Brooke's hands flew into the air. "You don't talk to guys about your babysitting jobs!" she scolded as the girls' classmates filed in for homeroom. "Geez! Okay, granted, maybe my tips didn't work out so well—though I think we've established that it's all in the execution—but you can't go around undoing all my hard work."

Elisabeth looked at her friend evenly. "Brooke, your work here is done."

"*Noooo*! I really want us to double-date to Spring Fling!"

Elisabeth looked at her quizzically. "Who are *you* going with?"

Brooke shrugged. "I haven't decided yet. But think about it: A double-date? *Soooo* much fun. Now, no more babysitting talk!"

Elisabeth giggled, still lost in her own thoughts. "You know what's weird? That wiping-the-invisible-smudge-off-his-face bit?"

"A classic. In the right hands."

"Well, Lance actually *did* have something on his face yesterday after tennis practice. It was a little piece of a leaf or something. So I wiped it off. And *that* time—maybe because it was a real thing and I wasn't acting like a freak—*that* time, it felt perfect."

Brooke studied her face for a moment. "Okay, good. It seems that maybe you're not completely hopeless," she said.

The girls began sorting their books on their desk as more classmates took their seats.

"Oh, by the way," Brooke asked, leaning closer, "how did tennis practice go? Think you'll make the team?"

Elisabeth considered the question and shrugged. "Probably not, but maybe. I did a lot better yesterday, when I started actually focusing on the ball rather than the imaginary smudges on Lance's face. Coach Morrison told me, 'Solid effort,' so . . . fingers crossed?"

Brooke held up her crossed fingers gamely.

"Thanks," Elisabeth said.

"Anything for you, girlfriend."

"Hey, I've been looking all over for you!"

Elisabeth glanced over her shoulder and saw Lance trotting toward her in the hall as she headed for her fifth-period class. Elisabeth slowed her pace as he caught up with her.

"Come with me!" he said, taking her arm and nudging her into a U-turn.

"Where are we going?"

"The gym. I heard Coach Morrison posted the team on the door."

Elisabeth's throat tightened. "Already? I thought he was making the announcement after school."

"We gotta hurry, before the bell rings," Lance said, walking faster.

Elisabeth swallowed hard, then tugged on Lance's arm to stop him in his tracks. Words bounced around in her head until she mumbled, "Go on without me."

He cocked his head to one side. "Why?" he asked as their classmates jostled past them.

Elisabeth bit her bottom lip. "Maybe I didn't make it."

Lance shrugged. "Maybe *I* didn't make it."

"I just . . . I'm too nervous to look. Go on without me and just, you know, give me a thumbs-up or a thumbs-down afterward in the hall."

Lance laughed. "And that would be better?"

She squeezed her books closer to her chest. "Maybe?"

"Aw, c'mon," he prodded.

Elisabeth shook her head and peered at him. "I was so awful those first couple of days."

He leaned closer. "But you came back. And you got better."

"It probably wasn't enough."

Lance offered her his hand. "Let's find out. Together."

She took a deep breath, then took his hand.

They'd find out together.

"Hey! Caldwell!"

Elisabeth turned back toward the gym and saw Coach Morrison coming out the door.

She smiled at him weakly. "Hi."

He waved her over. She and Lance headed back to where they'd just come from.

"Don't let this get you down," Coach Morrison told her, pointing with his thumb at the list on the door. The list of people who'd made the tennis team. The list Elisabeth wasn't on.

"I totally understand."

"It was a tough call," he continued. "I was really impressed with how you hung in there. I saw a big improvement yesterday. A *big* improvement."

She managed another smile. "Thanks."

"Keep at it, okay?" Coach Morrison said. "You can even practice with the team if you want to. Play as much as you can, come cheer us on at our matches, keep a sharp eye on the really good players—" He nodded toward Lance, still standing by her side. "—and by next spring, you should have an excellent shot at making the JV team."

"Thanks. Really."

"Lots of raw talent there," he said, walking past them and patting Elisabeth on the arm.

Elisabeth wrinkled her nose at Lance. "Bet he says that to all the losers."

"I thought that was great advice," Lance said, squinting into the sun. "Hang out with the team. Come to my matches. Watch and learn from the master."

She wrinkled her nose playfully. "Should I come to you for my lessons in modesty too?"

"I think you'll pick that up naturally, just by hanging around me."

"Well, *there's* an offer I can't refuse."

They laughed lightly.

"Hey," Lance said, shifting his weight nervously, "can I make you another offer you can't refuse?"

Elisabeth smirked slyly. "You can try me."

He shook a lock of hair off his forehead. "Spring Fling? Be my date?"

Birds chirped as nearby pine branches swayed in the breeze.

She smiled, then nodded.

"Deal."

Sitter Smarts

Think through potential problems and
have a game plan in place.

Chapter 10

". . . and I'll be home by six at the latest."

"Sounds good, Mrs. Stewart," Elisabeth said, straightening her blouse as Mrs. Stewart's little boys bustled excitedly on either side of her.

"They don't have sitters much," their mother said. "Usually, their older brother watches them if my husband and I have to be out of the house, but he's practicing with the cross-country team today. Do you know Will?"

"No, but my mom teaches him. She said he's really nice and really smart."

"Oh, your mother is such a wonderful teacher," Mrs. Stewart said, slipping her cell phone into her purse. "I sure hope these guys have her when they're in high school."

The boys were playing some kind of little game at Elisabeth's feet, tagging each other, then exploding into giggles with their hands over their mouths. They were cute kids—they looked like twins, other than Ethan being a little taller— and their hair was damp, as if their cowlicks had hastily been smoothed down. They wore matching T-shirts, and each had on a different color of shorts, everything squeaky-clean. The house was squeaky-clean too—bright and sunny, smelling of cinnamon, with a handful of bright-colored toys scattered about.

"Boys, please calm down," their mother said, then glanced apologetically at Elisabeth. "They're just so excited to have a visitor. And such a pretty one at that."

The boys giggled harder and Elisabeth felt her cheeks flush.

Their mom took a deep breath. "Okay, you've got my phone number, and my husband's and son's are on the fridge. Oh, wait, my son won't have his phone since he's running, but here's my husband's. Also, here's the number of the boys' pediatrician and the Poison Control Center. Of course, you know to call 9-1-1 in case of emergency?"

Elisabeth hesitated for a minute. *Was that a question?* she wondered. She finally nodded. "Oh, yes, ma'am. Plus, my mom's right down the street, so I'll have lots of backup if I need it." Elisabeth swallowed hard and dug her toes into her sneakers. Was that a stupid thing to say? Backup? Did it suggest she was expecting to need backup? ". . . not that I think I'll need it," she added nervously, twisting her fingers into pretzels.

"Oh, that's great to know, honey," Mrs. Stewart said. "You sound so mature. I know my boys are in great hands."

Mrs. Stewart bent down and kissed each of her sons on their cheeks, five shades rosier than they were when Elisabeth had arrived, thanks to nonstop rounds of tag and giggling.

"Please behave," she told them. Then she stood straight and gave Elisabeth a smile. "Cookies fresh out of the oven," she said, pointing to a jar on the counter. "Help yourself. Boys, you can have two each."

But the boys were zooming around again, back to their game. Elisabeth, apparently, was their base since neither of them ventured more than three feet from her ankles.

"We'll be fine," Elisabeth said, "I promise." Uh-oh. Did that sound overconfident? Like she didn't fully grasp what a big responsibility this was? "I mean . . ."

"Of course you will," Mrs. Stewart told her warmly. She grabbed her purse and headed for the kitchen door leading to the garage. "I'm locking this door on my way out, and the other doors are locked too. Plus, I'll close the garage door on my way out. If the boys want to play in the backyard, that's fine, as long as they stay inside the fence, of course; just don't lock yourselves out."

Elisabeth nodded, hoping her tensed shoulders weren't betraying her nerves. As nerve-wracking as the exploding eggs had been a few days earlier at Brooke's house, at least Elisabeth hadn't had to handle the situation alone. Suddenly, being left by herself with two little kids—two hyper little kids at that—seemed like a really big deal.

What if Elisabeth accidentally *did* lock them out of the house, for instance?

Then you'll walk twenty yards down the street and get Mom, she told herself testily.

And what if the boys wanted more than two cookies?

Then you'll say no. Quit worrying!

As Mrs. Stewart walked out the door, Elisabeth patted her back jeans pocket to make sure her phone was still there. She'd have it on her at all times, just in case. But everything would be fine.

Mrs. Stewart left to a chorus of bye-byes, then Elisabeth turned to face the little boys.

"Okay, guys," she said as they looked at her expectantly. *Now* they were still, like little soldiers waiting to take orders—or worse, like an audience waiting to be entertained. Mrs. Stewart hadn't even been out of the house five seconds, and the pressure was already killing Elisabeth.

She cleared her throat nervously. "Okay, guys, what do you usually do this time of day?"

The boys stared at her blankly. What a ridiculous question. In the first place, they didn't exactly carry day planners around, and in the second, they clearly had no intention of having a "usual" day. A babysitter was here! Woo-hoo! Time for adventure! Their big round eyes said it all: *Our expectations are huge. Amuse us.*

"Um," Elisabeth said, still twisting her fingers together. But then her eyes widened. "Jenga!" She'd taken Lance's advice and tossed the game into a plastic bag before leaving the house. "You guys ever played it?" she asked them, and they shook their heads. "Oh, you're gonna love it."

Please love it.

She walked over to the kitchen counter, retrieved the game from the bag, and led the boys to the kitchen table.

"Okay, we need to clear the table," she said then yelped as Eric began "clearing" it with a sweep of his outstretched arm.

"Not like that!" Elisabeth said. She grabbed his arm gently mid-sweep. "I mean, let's carefully pick up what's on the table and move it over to the counter."

The boys nodded agreeably and began helping her move the items . . . a vase of daisies, a set of place mats underneath the vase, a couple of high school textbooks. The boys handed the items one by one to Elisabeth, who placed them on the kitchen counter.

"Good job," she told them. "Now we can play."

They all took seats around the table, Ethan sitting on his knees with his forearms pressed against the table.

But Eric's little forehead barely cleared the table. "I can't see!" he whined.

"He has a baby chair," his brother told Elisabeth, pointing to a little upholstered seat that pressed into the table.

"I don't want the baby chair!" Eric protested, tears filling his eyes.

"It's okay, it's okay," Elisabeth said quickly, glancing around the room for a solution. Her eyes fell on the thick textbooks they'd just moved to the kitchen counter.

"Here," she told Eric, helping him off the chair as she placed the books in it. "These will make you nice and tall like your brother."

He beamed as he sat high in the seat.

"You're still littler than me," Ethan muttered, causing Eric to wail in protest.

"It's okay, it's okay," Elisabeth said. "Look, this game is pretty complicated. You've got to concentrate if you want to play."

"What does *complicated* mean?" Ethan asked.

"What does *concentrate* mean?" his little brother said.

"It means no crying or yelling allowed. You have to pay attention to the game if you want to win, and you can't do that if you're arguing with each other."

She felt her heart rate slow as she realized the logic was actually winning them over. The boys sat there like statues, their eyes glued to the Jenga tower that Elisabeth had begun constructing in the middle of the table.

"It might fall," Eric said wide-eyed as she added layer after layer.

"Your job is to make sure it doesn't," she told him. "Whoever makes it fall loses."

"I won't!" Eric said.

"He will," his brother told Elisabeth. "He's such a baby."

"Am not!"

Elisabeth's index finger flew to her lips. "You have to pay attention, remember?"

The boys grew silent again, and Elisabeth finished constructing the tower.

"Okay, guys: We'll each take a turn removing a stick from the tower . . . and you can't touch anything but the stick you're moving."

"Me first!" Eric said, plucking a stick from the top layer.

"You can't pick it from the top," Elisabeth told him. "Anywhere but the top."

"But then it'll fall," he said.

"That's why you have to concentrate and be careful. Here: Watch me."

She plucked a stick from the tower three rows deep.

The boys applauded. "Me next!" they cried in unison.

"Let's see," Elisabeth said. "We'll go in alphabetical order. That means whoever's name comes first in the alphabet goes first. Eric, the first letters in your name are E and R. Ethan, your first two letters are E and T. So Eric goes first."

"No fair!" Ethan wailed.

"You'll get to go first in the next game," Elisabeth promised him, and he nodded grudgingly. "Okay, Eric, time to take a stick out of the tower."

His hand hovered over the top for a minute, but then he lowered it. "Good job," Elisabeth told him.

He reached for the stick in the middle from the same stack where Elisabeth had removed hers.

"Maybe not the best plan," she told him quietly. "If a stick is already gone from the side on one stack, the tower will stay steadier if you pick the stick from the other side, rather than the one in the middle."

Eric reached for the stick on the opposite side, then used a pudgy hand to hold the tower in place as he began plucking it out.

"Remember, you can't touch anything but the stick you're trying to move," Elisabeth reminded him. Eric reluctantly moved his hand. As he began trying to remove the stick, she realized his little hand wasn't wide enough to reach both ends.

"Okay, you know what?" she said. "I have a better idea. I think you two should be a team. I'll have a turn, then you'll each have a turn, taking one of the sticks out together. Eric, you can move one end, and Ethan can move the other. But you know what teamwork means, right?"

Their eyes were glued on Elisabeth for the answer. "It means you have to work together. To get along. You can't say mean things to your teammate or call him names. That'll just make him mad and flustered, then you'll *both* lose when he messes up. So you have to support each other."

Again, she was stunned that they nodded agreeably. *Gosh, I'm pretty good!* she told herself. *I should be a judge!*

Elisabeth smiled as she remember Mima's list. She'd actually slipped it into her purse at the last second, and now she was glad she had. She wouldn't necessarily need the list, but she knew it would make Mima happy. And it made Elisabeth feel calmer, like her grandma was almost right there with her. Not hovering in the laundry room, but close enough.

And without even realizing it, she was already implementing Mima's tips: fairness, distraction, cooperation. Mima not only had solutions, she had anticipated the problems and taken the time to write them down for Elisabeth.

"Good job," she told the boys with a smile as they removed a stick, each of them lightly tugging on opposite ends to achieve their mutual goal. "That's what I call teamwork."

Sitter Smarts

Don't let kerfuffles devolve into full-scale meltdowns; nip kids' disagreements in the bud.

Chapter 11

Four games of Jenga later, Elisabeth and the boys decided they were ready for a change of scenery.

Ethan wanted to show her his favorite video, an exercise DVD featuring cartoon animals. The narrator walked the children through various motions: hopping like a bunny, reaching like an octopus, pouncing like a cat, slithering like a snake, freezing like an opossum.

Elisabeth scanned the family room to make sure there was nothing the boys could bump into or trip over, then popped in the video. She joined right in, with the boys prompting her to jump, hop, pounce, whatever. They all laughed hard, particularly when one of them would almost tip over while freezing like an opossum. By the end of the video, they were breathless and pink-cheeked but ready to do it again.

"You're the best babysitter ever!" Eric told Elisabeth, wrapping her in a hug.

"Aw. I bet you say that to all the babysitters."

She hit play and they completed the exercise video again, this time even goofier than before. By the time it was over, they were sprawled on the floor, laughing and panting lightly.

Suddenly Eric's eyes widened. "Uh-oh," he said as he jumped to his feet and vaulted for the bathroom.

After a minute, they heard the toilet flush and Eric emerged from the bathroom. "That was close," he said. *Bathroom reminders! Bathroom reminders!* Elisabeth scolded herself anxiously, nibbling a nail. Mima had suggested every forty minutes. Elisabeth wouldn't forget again.

Next the boys introduced Elisabeth to a couple of their board games. They occasionally spiraled into a spat—okay, fine, a *kerfuffle*—but

Elisabeth's distract-and-defuse skills kept away full-on meltdowns.

It was toward the end of game number three that Eric announced he was hungry.

"Me too," Ethan said, one of the few times all afternoon the boys had reached a consensus.

"Cookies?" Elisabeth suggested.

Ethan nodded heartily. "I'll go get them."

"No, that's okay," Elisabeth said as she hurried after him into the kitchen. She took the cookie jar, handed them one apiece, and said, "We need to eat them in here."

"Mommy lets us eat in front of the TV," Ethan told her.

"Not today. Babysitter rule."

"Says who?" Ethan challenged her.

Elisabeth's eyes flashed with sternness. "Says *me.*"

The boys stared at her solemnly.

Hmm! Apparently she *did* have a no-nonsense tone after all.

It took all of two seconds for Eric to inspect his cookie and begin whining, "Ethan's is bigger!"

"Is not!" Ethan insisted, but it kinda was.

"I'll give you a bigger one," Elisabeth said, digging into the jar and handing him another.

"Now his is bigger!" Ethan protested.

Elisabeth sighed. This could go on all day. "Eric, can I see your cookie for a second?"

Eric handed it to her and Elisabeth took a bite. "Now you're even."

Ethan exploded into laughter, but Eric's jaw dropped. "No fair! Now you have to eat a bite of *his* cookie too!"

Elisabeth squeezed her eyes shut. "Look: Both of you give me your cookies. I'll put them on the counter. Then each of you will close your eyes and reach into the jar. But whichever one you pick, that's it: That's your cookie. And you can't touch more than one. But after you're finished picking one, you can pick another one too, since your mom said that's how many you could have."

The boys looked at her suspiciously.

"*Or* you can eat the ones I picked for you," she said, her no-nonsense tone returning.

"We'll pick, we'll pick," Ethan said. Eric nodded in agreement.

"Okay, when's your birthday?" Elisabeth asked Ethan.

"May twenty-first."

"Eric? When's yours?"

"November sixth."

"Okay, Eric's is coming up first, so Eric, you get to pick a cookie first. Just one, then after Ethan picks one, you can both pick your second."

Ethan opened his mouth to protest, but Elisabeth said, "It's simple math." Somehow, this seemed to satisfy him.

Eric picked his cookie, then Ethan picked his. They repeated the process, then inspected their cookies.

Eric's bottom lip jutted out. "Ethan's are still bigger! At least *one* of them is."

Elisabeth slapped her palm against her fore-head. "You've got to be kidding me."

Eric started wailing. Ethan shouted over him, crying foul for refusing to abide by their agree-ment. Pretty soon, they were both in full-blown screech mode.

"Okay, whatever," Elisabeth grumbled to her-self, then did the least likely thing she ever expected to do. She started moonwalking.

Right there in the kitchen. The boys were oblivious at first, still screaming their grievances, but after a moment, their eyes locked on her. As she pressed one toe into the floor while sliding backward with the other, she repeated the move-ments and glided along the floor.

The boys stood in stunned silence for the first couple of moments then excitedly jumped up and down. "Teach me! Teach me!" they said in unison.

Elisabeth continued moonwalking a bit lon-ger—she wanted to distract them long enough to thoroughly defuse their meltdowns—then put a hand on her hip and looked at them evenly. "If you'll sit down nicely and finish your cookies, I'll teach you how to moonwalk."

"Yes!" the boys yelped, rushing to the kitchen table. As they munched their cookies happily, Elisabeth shook her head in disbelief. They were quiet! They were content! Elisabeth was a genius!

Well, okay. Mima's the one who had suggested the idea. But . . . it was all in the execution.

Elisabeth laughed lightly at the polka-dotted caterpillar on the television screen. "So what's this guy's name?" she asked the boys.

"Ethan? Eric?"

Elisabeth turned around in the chair and saw the little boys snoozing on the sofa. Wow. All that game-playing, exercising, snacking, and moonwalking must have worn them out. Their show had started barely ten minutes earlier, and they were out like a light. She took a deep breath.

Mrs. Stewart would be back within the hour, and if the boys spent most of that time napping, then she was home free.

She'd done it! She'd completed her first babysitting gig, and she'd done a rather fantabulous job of it, if she did say so herself. She smiled proudly and stood up, looking around to make sure she hadn't left any toys or games out of place. Nope. Everything looked great. Then she walked into the kitchen to clear any stray crumbs off the table. So she'd have to wait another year to try out for the tennis team? No problem! With Lance helping her practice, and with the babysitting jobs that were sure to fill her spare time now that she'd proven such a spectacular success, she had a feeling the year would fly by.

Oh, and she'd have her own money! And for now, at least, she wouldn't have to spend it on tennis gear. Her mind swam at all the possibilities—movies, basketball sneakers, mall visits, and pedicures with Brooke.

She glanced down at the cookies on the counter that the boys had rejected. Hmm . . . didn't mind if she did.

As she picked one up to take a bite, she heard the doorbell ring. She froze momentarily. It was silly to feel nervous; after all, the sun was still shining brightly outside. She never froze in her spot when her doorbell rang at home; it was ridiculous to feel apprehensive now.

She walked into the foyer, glancing into the family room on her way to make sure the boys were still sleeping. She peered through a blind and saw a young man she didn't know standing on the stoop. He was tall and skinny, wearing a sweaty T-shirt and shorts. Elisabeth estimated he was college-aged, maybe early twenties.

Well, *that* seemed kind of weird. It wasn't as if one of the boys' friends was dropping by to play. And she wouldn't have blinked an eye if the person at the door was a grown-up *lady*—one of their neighbors or one of Mrs. Stewart's friends.

But a man? Ringing the doorbell of a house where two little boys lived? And where both of the parents were out for the day? And why did he look so scruffy? If you were going to visit somebody, wouldn't you at least put on a clean shirt first?

Elisabeth's mind raced.

The best thing to do was ignore the doorbell. How important could the visit be? The guy probably had the wrong address anyway. He'd stand there for a minute, and when nobody answered, he'd take a second look at the house number and realize he was at the wrong place.

Yes. She'd just wait him out. She held her breath as she kept standing there, afraid that any motion or movement would reveal her presence.

After a couple of moments, the stranger rang the bell again. Then again.

Elisabeth's heart quickened. Why didn't he just go away?

Time seemed to stand still as she stood frozen in space, with nothing but the locked door separating her from the stranger.

Then she heard footsteps. She peeked out the blinds again and exhaled. He was leaving. Thank heaven! But as she watched him walk off the porch, her breath quickened again when she realized he was walking over to a window, checking to see if it was open.

Oh, no! Yes, all the windows were closed and locked . . . but what if they hadn't been? What did the stranger want? What was he doing here? Should she call 9-1-1 now?

She'd barely formed the thought as she realized he was moving from one window to another, then walking around the side of the house. Oh, no! She followed the sound of his footsteps, walking toward the back of the house. Elisabeth's eyebrows shot up. He'd opened the gate! He was in the backyard! She heard him walk to the back door, knock on it, and call out.

Oh gosh . . . *Oh gosh, oh gosh, oh gosh . . .*

Elisabeth took her phone from her back jeans pocket, gripped it, and prepared to call 9-1-1, peeking through the blinds facing the backyard.

Gasp! He'd seen her! When she peeked through the blinds, the stranger's eyes had locked directly onto hers! He'd seen her, and now he was waving his arms wildly at her.

Elisabeth swallowed hard again, then called out, "Could you come downstairs, Mr. Stewart? Quickly? Somebody's at the door."

The guy was still waving his arms. "Mr. Stewart!" she repeated, her voice louder this time as she called out for the boys' father, the man she *knew* wasn't upstairs. But the stranger outside didn't know that.

"Mr. Stewart, please come see who's at the door!" she called again, positioning her fingers over the keypad of the phone. Nine . . . one. . .

"Will!" Elisabeth gasped again as she real-ized Ethan had awakened and walked to the back of the house, opening the blinds to reveal the stranger at the door.

"Ethan!" she said, lurching toward him. But he was already opening the door. "Ethan!"

As the little boy opened the door, the stranger walked in.

Ethan looked at her innocently, startled by her frantic expression. "It's Will," he said.

Elisabeth ran her fingers through her hair. "Who?"

"Will," the stranger said. "His brother. I live here."

Elisabeth's hand flew over her mouth.

"Sorry to startle you," Will said. "I was at cross-country practice. I walked, so I didn't have my phone or my keys . . ."

Elisabeth opened her mouth to speak, but nothing came out.

"Is my dad home?" Will asked, walking toward the landing and peering curiously up the stairs.

"Daddy's not home," Ethan informed him.

"I . . . pretended," Elisabeth said, her galloping heart finally steadying. "I didn't know who you were—sorry about that—and I didn't want you to know I was here alone with the boys."

Will considered her words, then smiled. "Very smart," he said, nodding his head. "It totally worked. I was so confused."

"Sorry again . . ."

They glanced toward the garage as they heard the door open.

"Mommy's home!" Ethan cried triumphantly.

Whew. Mommy was home.

"I am *so* sorry." Mrs. Stewart squeezed Elisabeth's shoulder after hearing the story. "I truly thought I'd be home before Will. But I should have told you there was a chance he'd beat me back."

"No, no," Elisabeth insisted. "I should have realized. He just . . . he looks older than a teen-ager." She flashed a smile at Will. "No offense."

"Are you kidding?" Mrs. Stewart said. "You handled it beautifully! Not letting a stranger in, then pretending my husband was home, and getting ready to call 9-1-1? You were *so* clever!"

Elisabeth smiled, staring bashfully at her shoes. "Thanks. Still, it seems like a no-brainer that it was—"

Will held up a hand to stop her in mid-sentence. "You did good. Thanks for taking such good care of my little brothers."

Eric and Ethan started bouncing excitedly. "Mom," Eric said, "we played a new game! A game with a tower that tumbles down! And Elisabeth exercised with us! And we played—"

"Boys, boys!" Mrs. Stewart said, laughing. "I've got all evening to hear about your big day."

"Can Elisabeth babysit for us again?" Ethan asked.

Mrs. Stewart's eyes sparkled. "I sure hope so."

Sitter Smarts

After babysitting, pat yourself on the back for a job well done and make mental notes about what you can do better next time. Then on to the next job!

Chapter 12

"Oooooohhhh, I can't wait to help you shop for a dress!"

Elisabeth sighed. Now that she'd spilled the beans to her family about the Spring Fling, the "isn't that adorable" launch sequence had officially been activated.

"I remember Lance from last year's field trips," Elisabeth's mother continued as she passed a slice of pizza to Brooke. "Such a sweet boy! Of course, you're too young to date, but a school dance? Well, that's just—"

"Adorable?" Elisabeth suggested, making them all laugh.

Elisabeth's parents had decided a celebration was in order in light of her successful babysitting afternoon. As soon as Elisabeth had walked in the door, she'd blurted the story about Will trying to get into the house. Elisabeth's mom had hugged her and suggested that they call Brooke and Mima on the spot.

Now that Elisabeth had shared the news about the dance, she turned toward her grandmother and told her what happened with Will. Mima listened wide-eyed.

"Oh, honey, I'm so glad you took my advice!" she said.

"Mima, I took your advice about a zillion times today," Elisabeth told her, realizing that she couldn't wait to give her grandma's tips another whirl. The next job couldn't come soon enough. Babysitting was almost as fun as sports—and her parents didn't even have to pay for it!

"Come to find out, Mima," she said, "you give the best tips in the world."

"Well, I guess that balances out my *worst* tips in the world," Brooke said as they all laughed.

"Hey, I made enough money today to treat us to pedicures before the dance," Elisabeth told her.

"Oh, pedicures are our treat," her mom said.

"Pedicures!" her dad said. "What in the world is happening with my little jock?"

"You can be athletic and still have nice toes," Brooke responded.

"Plus, I have plenty of time for pedicures since I didn't make the tennis team," Elisabeth said.

"Are you kidding?" her dad responded. "I'm gonna get you out on those courts four or five days a week! We've got to get ready for next year."

"Well, technically, Lance has offered to help me with my game," Elisabeth said.

"Oh, has he now?" her dad grumbled teasingly. "We dads are so darn replaceable."

"Never," Elisabeth said, kissing his cheek.

"You know, I used to have a pretty decent tennis game myself," Mima said. "Maybe I could—"

"—give me some tips?" Elisabeth said. "Bring 'em on, Mima. Bring 'em on."

C. H. Deriso is an award-winning author of young-adult, middle-grade, and young children's books. Her upcoming young-adult novel, *Tragedy Girl*, will be published by Flux in early 2016. Deriso lives in North Augusta, South Carolina.

Glossary

defensive (di-FEN-siv)—if you are defensive, you feel and act as if you are being attacked or criticized

demonstrated (DEM-uhn-strate-ed)—showed other people how do something

desperate (DESS-pur-it)—willing to do anything to change a situation

exasperation (eg-ZASS-puh-ray-shun)—annoyance

execution (EK-suh-kyoo-shun)—the act or process of doing something

humiliating (hyoo-MIL-ee-ate-ing)—embarrassing

modesty (MOD-eh-stee)—the quality of being without vanity or boastfulness

preoccupation (pree-ok-yuh-PEY-shun)—something that distracts you

reluctantly (ree-LUHK-tuhnt-lee)—in a way that shows you don't want to do something

salmonella (sal-muh-NEL-uh)—any of a group of bacteria that are shaped like rods and can cause food poisoning, stomach inflammation, and typhoid fever in humans and other warm-blooded animals

sarcasm (SAR-kaz-uhm)—bitter or mocking words that hurt or make fun of someone or something

scenario (suh-NAIR-ee-oh)—a series of events that might happen in a situation

spectacular (spek-TAK-yuh-lur)—remarkable or dramatic

titanium (tye-TAY-nee-uhm)—a silvery-gray, light, strong metallic element found combined in various minerals

voluntary (VOL-uhn-ter-ee)—willing; not forced

Let's Talk!

1. Each chapter in the book begins with a babysitting tip that relates to the chapter. Choose a few of the tips and explain how they relate to what happens in the story.

2. If you had a chance to offer Elisabeth advice about either babysitting or boys, what tips would you include?

3. Do you think Elisabeth was well-prepared for her babysitting job? Use the text to support your answer.

Write About It!

1. Write a paragraph to compare and contrast Elisabeth with one of the following characters: Mima, Brooke, or Lance.

2. Rewrite the scene where Elisabeth pulls the string on Lance's shirt from his point of view. What is he thinking and feeling about the situation?

3. What piece of advice was the best and what piece of advice was the worst? Use examples from the text to support your answer.

Babysitting Basics

A lot of Mima's babysitting advice was designed to make the job safe. Safety is always your first priority when babysitting. Pay attention to what's happening around you and use your common sense. Stick to the rules and routines you have discussed with parents.

Plan for Emergencies

Before you perform any kind of child care, make sure you understand and can perform basic emergency procedures. Take a basic first-aid class. Know when and whom to call in an emergency.

Be Aware of Your Surroundings

Remember the key rules in babysitting. Pay attention and never leave children alone! Be aware of what's going on around you. Are there toys scattered around that a child could trip on? Are there small objects nearby that a toddler could choke on? Paying attention to these things will keep kids safe and happy.

Know the Routines and Rules

Children are happiest when they follow their normal routines. Discuss routines and preferences with a parent at the beginning of each job. You should know:

- What meals or snacks should children have? What foods are okay to eat?
- How much TV or electronics time is allowed? At what times?
- What TV shows are children allowed to watch? What video games are they allowed to play?
- What other activities are okay?
- Do the children need baths? What are the instructions for this?
- When is bedtime? What is the children's bedtime routine?

Excerpt from *You're Hired! Business Basics Every Babysitter Needs to Know* by Rebecca Rissman, published by Capstone Press, 2015.

Read more of The Babysitter Chronicles!

Bri's Big Crush

by Melinda Metz

Brianna Edwards has a big crush on the new boy, David Massey. So when Mrs. Massey asks her to babysit David's younger siblings, Bri sees it as her opportunity to connect with David. In order to get her crush's attention, Bri pretends that she shares his interests. Now she's so busy being someone she's not that she's forgetting to do all the special things that make her a great babysitter. When will Bri figure out that being herself is the best way to get the boy AND the babysitting job?

Kaitlyn and the Competition

by D. L. Green

Kaitlyn is a top-notch babysitter: she's organized, disciplined, and efficient. And she needs her regular babysitting gigs to pay for new clothes, bedroom decor, and of course, her cell phone bill. So when the Sweet family decides to replace her with a new, fun sitter named Doc, she's determined to beat her new competition . . . if only she could figure out who he is. But will Kaitlyn come to realize that even an experienced sitter like her can learn a thing or two from the new guy on the block?

Olivia Bitter, Spooked-Out Sitter

by Jessica Gunderson

With the start of seventh grade, Olivia's longtime friend, Beth, has found new interests and new friends. Olivia thinks if she could just afford the type of clothes that Beth now wears, maybe their friendship could be restored. Motivated by a need for cash, Olivia agrees to babysit for a family of four who recently moved to the neighborhood haunted house. Now she's not sure what's scarier: hearing countless creepy sounds or being responsible for four kids!

The fun doesn't
stop here!

Discover more at
www.capstonekids.com

- Videos & Contests
- Games & Puzzles
- Friends & Favorites
- Authors & Illustrators

Plus, find cool websites and more books like
this one at www.facthound.com.

Just type in the Book ID: 9781496527578
and you're ready to go!